Nigel West, the █████████████████████
Quarterly, has w██████████████████████
works on the sub████ ██████ ████ ██████.
He was voted 'The Expert's Expert' by the
Observer and is an acknowledged authority in
his field. In writing *Murder In The Lords*, and
his previous parliamentary whodunnit *Murder
In The Commons*, Nigel West has drawn on his
experience as a police officer in Westminster and
as a government back-bencher.

Critical acclaim for *Murder In The Commons*:

'A fiendishly complicated murder story . . . with
a lot of information about Commons procedures'
Sunday Express

'Solidly crafted plot, but main fascination lies in
insider's exposure of parliamentary anachronisms and how's your father' *The Sunday Times*

Also by Nigel West

Non fiction

Spy! (*with Richard Deacon*)
MI5: British Security Service Operations, 1909–45
MI6: British Secret Intelligence Service Operations,
1909–45
A Matter of Trust: MI5, 1945–72
Unreliable Witness: Espionage Myths of World War II
The Branch: A History of the Metropolitan Police
Special Branch
GARBO (*with Juan Pujol*)
GCHQ: The Secret Wireless War
Molehunt
The Friends: Britain's Postwar Secret Intelligence
Operations
Games of Intelligence
Seven Spies Who Changed the World
Secret War: The Story of SOE
The Faber Book of Espionage

Fiction

The Blue List
Cuban Bluff

Murder In The Commons

Murder
In The Lords

Nigel West

HEADLINE

First published in 1994
by Macmillan London Limited

First published in paperback in 1995
by HEADLINE BOOK PUBLISHING

10 9 8 7 6 5 4 3 2 1

ISBN 0 7472 4412 X

Printed and bound in Great Britain by
Cox & Wyman Ltd, Reading, Berks

HEADLINE BOOK PUBLISHING
A division of Hodder Headline PLC
338 Euston Road
London NW1 3BH

To Richard and Susan
who know where at least
one of the bodies is buried.

Contents

Chapter One	Their Lordships' Consideration	1
Chapter Two	Her Ladyship	23
Chapter Three	The Viscount	53
Chapter Four	The Life Peer	81
Chapter Five	The Ninth Earl	115
Chapter Six	The Duke	141
Chapter Seven	The Life Peeress	167
Chapter Eight	The Marquess	189
Chapter Nine	The Librarian	203
Chapter Ten	Black Rod	221

Chapter One

Their Lordships' Consideration

It is very rare that the decorum of the House of Lords is disturbed. The five golden knights, guarding the royal coat of arms over the huge empty throne, demand solemnity. It happened once in recent times when a group of lesbian campaigners abseiled into the chamber from the public gallery. With characteristic stoicism their Lordships ignored the distraction and continued their debate. There was a similar murmur of comment across the red leather benches when ashen-faced attendants spread the news of a murder in the Not Content Lobby to one of the dead man's colleagues standing at the bar. Philip North, a visitor from the Commons, was close by, listening to the debate, when the commotion began.

It was mid-afternoon and North had been leaning against the ornate barrier that separated their Lordships' guests and Members of the Lower House from the rows of scarlet benches. By a quaint but uncomfortable custom MPs were not allowed to be seated here, although there were more than fifty chairs in the area known as the Bar of the House. If they wished to sit down they were obliged to climb up a small staircase to the narrow, cramped gallery overlooking the chamber that was specifically reserved for them. North, with his six foot two frame, was quite incapable of squeezing into the tiny space for any length of time, but he was keen to hear the debate. Nor was his desire to listen to their Lordships so unusual; it was universally recognized that the standard of debate in the Upper House was far higher than in the lower chamber where 648 party hacks parroted the party line with scarcely an original thought between them. Certainly the Commons was not a place where opinions were changed or minds were swayed by intellectual exchange. The whips ruled and unless there was an appalling breakdown among the Government's business managers, the results of each division were unsurprising and entirely predictable. The exceptions were those rare occasions when Members were allowed a free vote, when the authority of the Government was not under challenge. The committee stage of the War Crimes Bill was just such an occasion.

The issue of whether elderly *émigrés* from Eastern Europe should be put on trial for atrocities committed abroad during the Second World War was one that had raised passions on all sides, and was considered a matter of conscience. Yet these votes, on individual clauses and amendments, were not entirely free, for what was known disparagingly as the payroll vote had been whipped to support the Government. The 'payroll' were the 160 Members on the Government benches who had received patronage, either a ministerial appointment or a junior post such as Parliamentary Private Secretary, the first rung on the ladder of preferment. A vote by an MP against the wishes of his Chief Whip would require resignation and a return to the furthest of the back benches. As for Philip North, his voting intentions were governed not by any considerations of ambition, for he was generally regarded as too much of a maverick for promotion, but by the arguments presented on the floor of the House, and by his constituents. For the peers, the lack of electioneering humbug, and constituents to appease had always been a justification of the Upper House.

North's inclination was to leave the old Nazis in peace, in the hope that their troubled consciences would give them sleepless nights until they were held to account when they met their maker. Why bother to mount lengthy investigations, take evidence from a diminishing number of eye-witnesses with not entirely reliable memories, and hold expensive trials, all to send a geriatric defendant to prison for what could only be a relatively short period? North himself was too young to have had any personal experiences of the Second World War and had been born scarcely in time for the end of the Korean conflict, so he regarded the calls for retribution to be verging on the unhealthy. Why open old wounds, especially at such a sensitive time when European unity was supposed to be high on the agenda?

When the Bill was first published North had

received an eloquent letter from a shopkeeper constituent who revealed himself as the local stringer of the *Jewish Chronicle*. Although North had met him a couple of times at meetings of the chamber of trade in Ashburton, it had not occurred to him that he was Jewish. Indeed, his tale was one not of personal hardship but of the loss of his family in the Holocaust after he and his brother had been sent to safety in England. After the war his brother had returned to Czechoslovakia to search for their family, and all he had heard was of the horror of street round ups, of mass deportations, and of the extermination camps. Should all this be forgotten? Should those responsible be allowed to exploit a loophole in Britain's nationality laws to escape the justice they would have received if they had remained in their native countries?

The point that had altered North's opinion had been a simple one. If there is a time limit on murder, what is it? 'If you are saying that a murderer doesn't have to worry about being prosecuted if he can get away with his crime after a certain period, tell me,' the businessman had demanded. 'Is it ten, twenty, forty years? Let me know, because I've often been tempted by my mother-in-law to commit a homicidal act.' North had recognized his position. His views had hardened when he had heard the harrowing speeches of Jewish Members from both sides of the House during the Bill's Second Reading. Each had his own horror story to recount, and the debate had been concluded by an eloquent speech from Merlyn Rees, the former Labour cabinet minister who had described

4

in graphic detail some of the camps he had visited in Germany immediately after the surrender. The chamber had received each contribution in absolute silence, as though the blue carpet had absorbed every extraneous sound, with just the occasional gasp of shock to emphasize the perceptibly electric atmosphere. It had been a great Parliamentary occasion, on a topic that had divided the House right across the usual party differences.

The contrast with their Lordships could scarcely have been greater. Whereas emotion ruled the day in 'the other place', as their Lordships referred to the Commoners, it was the lawyers who commanded most attention in the ornate, throne-dominated chamber. The Commons was devoid of unnecessary decoration, whereas the Upper House was a riot of colour. The carved walls were covered with coats of arms, and the statues of the eighteen barons who had forced the Magna Carta upon a reluctant King John watched the proceedings carefully. The Lord Chancellor lolled on the deep red cloth of the Woolsack, listening attentively as peer after peer criticized the Bill. The seat, with just a small backrest on the top of the Woolsack, was notoriously uncomfortable but no serious attempt had been made to exchange it for a more sensible chair. Judges had sat on wool, brought from every corner of the Empire to demonstrate the wealth of the land, since the reign of Edward III, and tradition meant everything in Their Lordships' chamber. Between the two vast candlesticks which flanked the throne were the three broad steps on which several figures squatted, their ears straining to catch every word of the speeches.

Ranged against the legal big guns were the trembling voices of the Chief Rabbi from his position on the cross-benches, who insisted the Bill was about justice, not vengeance, and the suave Lord Tremaine from the Government benches who suggested a compromise solution: why not deport the suspected war criminals to those countries seeking their extradition? Having once been the Employment Secretary in a Conservative administration, Tremaine knew all about steering a middle path and finding remedies agreeable to all.

The chamber was unusually full, for the debate was not without its constitutional significance. The Bill had already been passed by the Commons and if it were rejected by the Lords, as Tremaine pointed out with his characteristic diplomacy, the Government might invoke the provisions of the Parliament Act which would have the effect of placing the measure on the Statute Book with inordinate speed. Would the peers defy the elected Commoners? The bulky Government Chief Whip could be seen moving to and from his seat on the red leather front bench, darting in and out of the chamber, presumably to gauge the likely outcome of the division later that night. Under some circumstances he could rely on the 'backwoodsmen', the fifty or so rare attenders from the Tory ranks who would heed a plea for loyalty from the party whips and leave their estates in the shire counties to repel unwelcome Opposition sorties, but this was an issue where traditional loyalties could not be counted upon. If the matter at stake was one of putting elderly gentlemen with difficult pasts into the dock at the Old Bailey, the Chief Whip had a shrewd idea of how several hundred others might be expected to vote.

For a few moments, as a cloud dulled the afternoon light flooding through the tinted glass in the roof of the chamber, North considered the startling news of Lord St Oliver's death. Lord St Oliver was another of the Lords' more colourful Members. One of the ill-fated recipients of Wilson's patronage in the Labour prime minister's notorious resignation honours list, he had served a short prison sentence for fraud when his media empire collapsed in 1983. St Oliver's reappearance in the Lords after his release from Rudgate Open Prison had caused much embarrassment on the Labour benches, but the failed tycoon was perfectly entitled to resume his place in the Lords. Utterly impervious to the pleas from his former friends to stay away from the Palace of Westminster, Sigi had started where he had left off and had begun to rebuild his publishing firm with money from an American heiress who believed him to have been the victim of an anti-Semitic conspiracy, a bizarre interpretation of events that Sigi had endorsed and probably inspired.

Sigi was one of the most unpopular Members of the Lords, thought North, and few would mourn his passing. His ruthless business methods had made him many enemies and left a string of victims. Whereas several peers had experienced brushes with the law at some point in their career, their colleagues had always been generous when the person who had erred had demonstrated some humility and contrition. Neither adjective would ever have been applied to Sigi, who could not even count on support from any of his three ex-wives. Two had returned to the United States, their wealth somewhat diminished, while his most recent ex, a rich widow from Huddersfield, had abandoned him when the tabloids had tracked her errant husband down to a motor yacht moored in the harbour at Sliema in Malta, which the lecherous peer had been sharing with a nanny young enough to be his granddaughter.

Sitting on the cross-benches only a few feet away, North spotted the historian Lord Staveley, his pebble-thick glasses balanced on his prominent nose, and knew that he would not shed any tears for Sigi, the man he blamed as the architect of his disgrace. St Oliver had persuaded Staveley to give his endorsement to the notorious *Himmler Diaries*. The diaries had subsequently been proved forgeries, and Staveley's name had become a by-word for academic incompetence; he had been forced to retire from his prestigious history chair and he now spent a large part of his time in the Lords.

As North scanned the benches further he spotted another victim of Sigi's mischief. Tony Rendell, sitting two rows behind Tremaine, had resigned from the Commons after being caught up in a call-girl scandal.

A junior minister at the time, he had met the woman at one of Sigi's parties and had employed her as a research assistant so as to conceal their affair. Reportedly, MI5 had learned of the relationship and after a suitably discreet warning, conveyed by the Secretary to the Cabinet, Rendell had sacked the woman who had promptly sold her tale to the *People*. The lurid headlines over pictures of the scantily clad prostitute, posed in what was described as a love-nest in Redcliffe Gardens, had caused an entirely predictable sensation, not so much about the 'kiss-and-tell' nature of the 'world exclusive', but rather because of the revelation that Rendell had enjoyed the occasional joint, and allegedly had made unusual sexual demands on other hookers.

Rendell had been stoic. His refusal to pass the blame had brought him considerable support. There had been no cries of invasion of privacy, no calls for control of the press. Instead there was a short, dignified letter of resignation to the Prime Minister and a single, awkward television appearance. He had applied for the Stewardship of the Chiltern Hundreds, and five years later had inherited his father's title. He had parted from his long-suffering wife and had turned his hand to military history, writing the best analysis of the Ardennes Offensive, as well as the definitive biography of Sir Desmond Morton, Churchill's wartime intelligence adviser, and for the past two years he had been engaged on a revisionist study of Field Marshal Montgomery. If it had not been for Sigi's propensity for what had once been termed 'popsies' in polite society, contemplated North, Rendell might still be a member of the Government. Indeed, he would most probably be a senior member of the Cabinet and very likely a candidate for the premiership, notwithstanding the handicap of having been educated at Harrow and Christ Church.

North turned to leave the chamber, but as he pushed through the handsomely carved double-doors his path was blocked by the trim figure of ex-Sergeant Major Laurie Cox, one of the twenty-three stalwarts known in the Lords by the title of Doorkeepers, who guarded the traditions of both Houses.

'I'm sorry, Mr North,' he said firmly. 'No one's to leave the chamber. There's been a terrible incident. I have my instructions.'

North paused for a moment. 'Is it true Lord St Oliver has been murdered?' he enquired.

'It's not for me to say, sir,' he replied, his face granite hard, his eyes opaque and immobile. 'I'm afraid you'll have to wait until the police have arrived.'

The younger man paused for a moment. 'On whose authority? I have to return to the Commons.'

The Doorkeeper's orders had been issued by Black Rod, but North was a Commoner. The Gentleman Usher of the Black Rod had no right to impede a Member of the Lower House, and for all he knew there could be a division at any moment. Nowadays he took little notice of the business in the Commons, for he had no reason to. He quickly recognized the implications of preventing an MP from pursuing his

Parliamentary business. 'Well, I'm sure you can go,' he admitted with some uncertainty. 'I'll have to tell the police, of course.'

'You do that,' murmured North, as he strode across the lobby and past a milling group of tourists who were arguing with the uniformed constable on duty at the desk by the set of double doors that divided the Peers' Lobby from the Peers' Corridor and the Central Lobby. North glanced at the dozen or so faces in the crowd, and recognized the tallest; he filed away the information in his mind. It was Viktor Strelets, the London correspondent from the TASS news agency. How odd for a hard-line old Party *apparatchik* like Strelets to be reporting from this bastion of class and inherited privilege. On second thoughts, he reconsidered with a wry grin, perhaps it was not so strange after all. Surely the House of Lords was as close to the Kremlin as one was likely to find in Moscow?

The following morning North got up early, leaving fast asleep his girlfriend Debbie Buxton with whom he shared his mansion flat and his mid-week. Weekends were saved for his constituency of Biddecombe, his understanding wife Cassandra, who worked as a solicitor in Exeter, and their daughter. It was an arrangement that worked to the satisfaction of all, except Debbie when he was obliged to rise early. She was tall, slim and independent, and showed no sign of resenting the MP's double life. Although the norm in Paris, where such infidelities were part of the culture and accepted as the way of life, behaviour of this kind had cost Senator Gary Hart a Presidential nomination in the US, and took its toll among members of the British Cabinet. For unambitious backbenchers like North, the liaison was an inevitable consequence of the dichotomy of family life in the country and Parliamentary pressure in London. The whips remained tolerant for as long as the tabloids exercised caution, and Cassandra's grasp of the laws of libel would ensure the silence of the journalists until some lapse in discretion occurred. Apart from a mischievous item in the Londoner's Diary column of the *Evening Standard*, which Cassandra did not read, the names of North and his girlfriend had been linked only once, in a photograph published in *Hello!*, when they both attended a gallery opening.

North sipped a solitary breakfast of frozen grapefruit juice while leafing through the news reports of the murder of Lord St Oliver, the first such incident within the precincts of the Palace since the assassination of Airey Neave in 1979.

During his extraordinary life Sigi had given the newspapers much to write about. His origins were to be found somewhere before the war in Lithuania but other immigrants from the Baltic states never succeeded in determining his antecedents. Certainly his family was not one of the well-to-do Jewish merchants of Kaunas or Riga. When reporters had probed this part of his life Sigi had always become vague, stating only that his earlier existence, before his arrival in Dorset at a Displaced Persons' camp, had been too painful to recall. He had at various times mentioned the Warsaw ghetto, and had once boasted about having walked most of the way across Europe in his youth. His documented past, available in every Fleet Street cuttings library, followed the story of the farm labourer who found a job on a McAlpine building site and was promoted to foreman. As one of the construction family had later joked to him on the day he took his seat in the Lords, 'If you had stayed with us you could have been a project manager by now.' By the time Sigi had started converting ex-RAF Nissen huts to industrial use he had dropped the last part of his surname and changed it by deed poll from Rosenbaum to Rose. He was an early promoter of frozen vegetables and later swapped his expanding food storage business for domestic electrical equipment. He was briefly a backer of Rolls-Razor, John Bloom's ill-fated kitchen appliance manufacturer, before switching to printing plant. He clashed with Robert Maxwell's British Printing Corporation and later conceded in an unfortunate off-the-cuff remark which was an uncharacteristic attempt at modesty, that 'the better man had won'.

Sigi's transformation into a London publisher came after he had already amassed a sizeable fortune. The firm of Truscott & Sweeting was well established if rather staid, with a not unimpressive list of non-fiction authors who invariably recouped their modest advances. Sigi had seen the company as his entrée into English society and had thrown a series of glitzy publication parties to mark his arrival. To finance his purchase of several best-selling novelists he sold T & S's principal asset, the magnificent listed property in Poland Street, and moved his editors into three floors of a modern block in Lambeth, which also accommodated several borough council offices. To the dismay of his staff, Sigi himself started to commission books from new authors, mainly politicians he had invited to his soirées, offering extravagant advances that could not possibly be justified in commercial terms, even if the publicity generated was impressive. His most famous coup was to persuade a glamorous ITN newscaster to write a semi-autobiographical book on sex and travel for an advance rumoured to be well into six figures. The story appeared in every newspaper diary column and Sigi knew he was a hot property when the crusty former Chancellor of the Exchequer in the Labour Government agreed to write his warts-and-all memoirs. These were not to be another version of *The Crossman Diaries*, but rather a more anecdotal account of internecine conflict and the struggle between Left and Right in the Labour Cabinet.

Sigi's star began to wane after the *Himmler Diaries* fiasco. Then he ran into trouble with his purchase of the rights to Frank Mitchell's autobiography. Actually ghosted by a former *Daily Mirror* crime reporter, who had been one of the few journalists ever to have been sacked by the newspaper group for concocting bogus bills to inflate his expenses, the book was purported to have been written by the 'mad axeman' while still an inmate in Broadmoor. Mitchell, an unrepentant psychopath who had been an enforcer for the Kray

gang, had cheerfully admitted in print to having butchered half a dozen underworld figures, including
Jack 'the hat' McVittie. Sigi believed he had made a
brilliant purchase until the Archbishop of Canterbury
made an outspoken attack on those who sought to
reward and glamorize criminals. Suddenly the T & S
blockbuster was transformed into a political target
and the Home Secretary announced new legislation
to prevent convicted criminals from capitalizing on
their misdeeds. Sigi's inelegant attempts, first to justify the payment of what he had claimed was a modest
sum to Mitchell, and then to feign ignorance when
details of the various contracts emerged, left him iso-
lated. *Private Eye* disclosed the identity of the book's
real author, and a *Sunday Times* feature article
researched in meticulous detail by Barrie Penrose
revealed that some of the more gruesome aspects of
Mitchell's tale could not possibly be true. Indeed, one
particularly vicious killing claimed by Mitchell, the
hitherto unsolved murder of a Maltese pimp in Soho,
whose dismembered body had been found in Epping
Forest, could not have been the handiwork of the 'mad
axeman', who had been serving three years in Dart-
moor at the time. The *Mirror* journalist who had
embroidered Mitchell's story, and according to the
special hospital's records had only visited him twice,
went into hiding. Penrose's exposé set Sweeting &
Truscott on a decline and St Oliver's parties were
boycotted by the glitterati who had previously been
so pleased to wolf his canapés and quaff his vintage
Krug.

The collapse of T & S, and then of Sigi himself, was precipitated by another example of the proprietor's failing judgement. He chose to defend a libel action brought by the skipper of a U-boat accused of having machine-gunned in the water the survivors of a merchant ship torpedoed off the Gold Coast in 1943. Neither Sigi nor the author, who aspired to the chair of modern history at Manchester University, entertained any notion that the *Kriegsmarine* officer had survived the war but, aged seventy-seven, he emerged from southern Ontario in good health to bring an action for defamation. Unwisely, Sigi opted to ignore the advice of his barrister, who urged him to settle as the action was impossible to defend. The case was heard before a jury, and the highly decorated plaintiff emerged victorious, having won what was then record damages. After the verdict was returned, Sigi discovered that his libel insurance would only cover the amount of damages his lawyer had advised him to settle for. Suddenly T & S was in terminal financial trouble, and when the Official Receiver scrutinized the company's records Sigi was charged with trading while insolvent and conspiracy to defraud his shareholders. Shortly before his trial was due to open Sigi disappeared, only to be found in Malta and ignominiously escorted back to Heathrow by two Fraud Squad detectives. The humiliation of the First Baron St Oliver was completed when he was sentenced to a three-year stretch, but the rotund little publisher had expressed no remorse and had told the waiting media hordes that the rest would do him some good and, rather more ominously, that he would be back in the saddle soon, for they had not seen the last of Sigi Rose. True as his word, he was back in the Lords within a week of his release from Rudgate, and soon afterwards became a regular attender at meetings of the Penal Affairs Parliamentary Group, a committee drawn from the Lords and Commons, and resumed his claim for the £97 daily attendance allowance paid to all Members of the Lords who call in at the Palace of Westminster.

North's musings were interrupted by the telephone. It was Detective Chief Inspector Young, who was heading the St Oliver murder inquiry, from an incident room set up in Westminster Hall. The senior CID officer unceremoniously demanded North's immediate presence in his temporary office. The men had worked together, a year or so earlier, tracking the killer of a Labour MP, and the policeman consequently dispensed with formalities.

'How dare you excuse yourself from the scene of a crime?' he demanded now. 'Do you realize you risk prosecution for, at the very least, obstruction?'

'I hesitate to remind you of the unique status of the Palace of Westminster,' replied North, unruffled by Young's threat, 'but I can hardly be a suspect in this case. I scarcely knew the man and I have a job to perform. As you can see, I haven't fled the country, I merely strolled across to the other chamber to fulfil my duties to my constituents.' As his words emerged, he could not suppress a chuckle. The morning had not started so badly after all.

'There'll be no arguments with the Speaker this time,' announced the detective, ignoring North's remarks. 'I had a meeting last night with the Lord Chancellor and I have his complete authority to conduct this investigation in any manner I wish. Protocol be damned; you're liable to be facing charges. I want to see you now ... in my office. I'm in Westminster Hall.'

North hesitated, considering for a moment that perhaps the detective was making a serious threat. 'Do you really mean that? Am I really a suspect?'

'You and one thousand, two hundred and eighteen others, not including the staff in the Lords. I need your help and I want it now ... down here ... please.' The politeness was an afterthought.

'Was that how many people were in the Lords yesterday?' asked North, puzzled by the figure.

'No. That's how many Members there are of the House of Lords, or so Lord Mackay tells me. From the few preliminary enquiries we've been able to make, it seems that Sigismund St Oliver was not Mr Popularity and most, if not all of them, have a motive for seeing him dead.'

'And how did he die? The papers say he was stabbed.'

'Come down here and find out for yourself. Phil ... this is a Godawful mess and you're needed, now. Get yourself here before I send someone to arrest you.'

Forty minutes later North climbed the steps at St Stephen's Entrance and was nodded past the queue of visitors by the police sergeant on duty at the heavy oak doors. The walk from St Stephen's Entrance, through St Stephen's Hall, where the Commons had met until the fire of 1834, to the Central Lobby, was an unforgettable experience, the grandeur of the surroundings so steeped in history never failing to overwhelm the thousands of visitors who walked through every day, but the MP, like his colleagues, took the cathedral-like magnificence of the Gothic architecture for granted. He had made the short journey from his mansion flat off Lord North Street by foot, and on the way had pondered his uneasy relationship with the policeman from Rochester Row station. They had first met under difficult circumstances, following the death of Alun Rees MP. Young and his assistant, Detective Inspector Shawcross, had blundered into the Palace of Westminster to pursue an ingenious and resourceful murderer and had nearly lost their quarry. The Speaker had been outraged by their indiscreet press briefings and their confrontational style which, while no doubt effective with demented serial killers or homicidal inadequates seeking their warped revenge on society, had not cut much ice with ministers of the Crown or Government whips. North had been drafted in to smooth over the wrinkles, not least because he had himself spent seven years in the Metropolitan Police, albeit with the rank of Special Constable. At first Young had resented the imposition by the Speaker of the youthful MP, but the Parliamentary maverick had managed to steer the detectives through the minefield of procedure and standing orders to gain the police a modicum of co-operation and the two had developed a rapport. Young, however, had not lost his contempt for what he had regarded as the anachronisms of the Palace of Westminster which he considered unreasonable obstacles in the way of catching a criminal, albeit an uncommon one.

The Lucan inquiry had been Young's first baptism into the unfamiliar world of gambling toffs and high-living courtesans, and it had been an unhappy experience. The aristocratic fringes on which he had been obliged to operate had been new territory and he had been at a disadvantage. With the Rees case, North had been the diplomat who had tactfully defused the awkward situations that had developed, calming the atmosphere when the tension had risen. The collaboration had resulted in a good conviction and North had met Young twice since, once to celebrate the outcome of the Old Bailey trial, and more recently a long lunch to discuss the idea of writing a book about the investigation. The project had come to nought but, mused North, perhaps this was another opportunity. Sigi St Oliver had been a larger than life character, and a gory murder in the Lords would have the media vultures flying around the carcass.

As he bypassed the security search area which routinely screened all visitors to the Palace Philip North marvelled at the transformation of Westminster Hall. Sometimes described as Europe's first shopping mall, where markets were held in medieval times, it was, with what was left of the Jewel Tower, the oldest building in the precincts, its magnificent carved oak roof testimony to the skill of Richard II's designers who had created a structure built to last, and one that had survived the fire that had destroyed virtually all the rest of the palace in 1834. Charles I had been tried in the Hall, and Churchill had lain in state there. President Reagan had addressed both Houses of Parliament here, as had the present monarch upon the celebrations of the Glorious Revolution. Tennis balls belonging to Henry VIII, the last sovereign to live in the palace, had been found among the hammer-beam rafters during routine maintenance, and the vast area reeked history, marked by brass plaques set into the cold, pitted flagstone floor. Now, at the far end, by the staff canteen which overlooked New Palace Yard, several hundred square feet had been cordoned off and the police had improvised an incident room. Inside it, North was offered a seat by Detective Chief Inspector Young. The older man gave his visitor a wan smile.

'So as to satisfy your curiosity at the outset,' he said curtly, 'Lord St Oliver was not really knifed to death, as you described it. He was more like cut to death. His throat was cut with such ferocity that he was virtually decapitated.'

Chapter Two

Her Ladyship

North swallowed hard as he heard the detective describe St Oliver's injuries.

'According to the pathologist's preliminary report, the victim was seized from behind by a taller, right-handed assailant who drew a long sharp knife or razor across the throat at a downwards angle, from left to right, severing the windpipe. Then the cutting motion was repeated, perhaps five or six times, inflicting deeper wounds.

'St Oliver probably died of loss of blood, which spurted upwards and sideways from the carotid artery, or maybe shock. He certainly died without uttering a sound. The body then slid to the floor, the upper torso leaning against a pillar in an alcove in one of the voting lobbies, the head resting at right angles on the left shoulder but concealed behind a heavy red velvet curtain. If the carpet had not also been red, the place would have looked like an abattoir.

St Oliver may have been a short little bastard, but
he had plenty of blood.'

Young looked up from his notes for a moment. 'And,
incidentally, this will interest you. Something really
quite unusual, I imagine. His blood was red, not blue.'

North gave a weak smile as Young continued. 'As
the attacker probably remained behind St Oliver
while he died, he may not necessarily have been
covered in blood, although there is bound to be considerable forensic evidence recovered from his or her
clothes. There are smudged footprints on the carpet,
and the killer must have left the scene quite blood-
stained. There is little chance of latent prints on the
stonework or curtain material, and none have been
recovered from the handle on the door inside the
alcove which leads to the chamber. Until we have
the more detailed report, I'd say we are looking for a
male, at least five foot eight tall, and right-handed.
From the severity of the wounds we can deduce that
this was a frenzied attack and the killer is most likely
a psychopath who might strike again. Now you can
tell me about access and motive.'

Slightly numbed, North asked, 'You're ruling out
a woman?'

'Not necessarily. Although the attack happened in
the Not Content Lobby, that does not exclude a
woman who perhaps opportunistically followed St
Oliver into it, possibly in the expectation that they
would be alone for a few moments. As for the height
of the assailant, there are plenty of women taller
than St Oliver. He was attacked from behind, so it is

probable that if he was standing with his back to her, he would never have known his attacker was a woman. That, of course, is speculation.'

'Who found the body?' asked North.

'You'll hardly credit this. It was a bishop. The Bishop of Donnington,' replied the detective.

North nodded. 'He's one of the Lords Spiritual. There are twenty-six bishops and archbishops entitled to sit in the Lords.'

Young arched an eyebrow and looked sceptical. 'Really? Well, Donnington raised the alarm by telling one of the Doorkeepers in the Peers' Lobby. He's called Cox and he took a look for himself and then told the uniformed sergeant on duty at the desk. As a result we know that both Donnington and Cox's hands touched the handle on the door. We estimate that Donnington must have found the body within a very few minutes of death. Anything up to ten.'

'How do you calculate the ten minutes?' asked the MP.

'The alcove is only used by the *Hansard* shorthand notetakers. Apparently they slip in and out of the chamber about every twelve or fifteen minutes. Donnington spotted the body before the lady from *Hansard* had been relieved, so that makes it ten minutes . . . at the outside.'

'Does that mean Donnington and Cox are suspects too?' queried North, as he pondered the implications.

'Nobody's ruled out. We won't know about motive until they've been interviewed, which will happen shortly – Cox is already waiting outside – but they both had the opportunity. Donnington discovered the body but says he never touched it. Cox was on duty within a few yards of the Not Content Lobby, but was behind the doors of the Peers' Lobby so had no clear vision of the alcove. Nevertheless, he could easily have slipped away from his post for a moment or two. The attack would not have lasted more than a few seconds.'

'But are there other, more likely candidates?' ventured the MP.

'Well, you tell me,' replied the detective. 'If the killer is a maniac, as suggested by the wounds, it may have been a motiveless assault, but a voting lobby in the House of Lords is an unusual place for a psychopath to select a random victim. Bearing in mind the controversial nature of the victim, we must assume, for the time being, that St Oliver was a deliberately chosen target. At the present time,' he said rather pedantically, as though he were rehearsing his appearance in the inevitable press conference, 'I am working on the basis that this was a cold-blooded and calculated homicide. St Oliver had done time and seems to have been disliked by everyone, but there was nothing in his behaviour immediately prior to the incident to suggest that he knew he was in danger. We'll know more when we finish searching his flat but yesterday he had lunch with a peer in the Lords Dining Room and then took his seat. There were four hundred and five peers known to be in the Lords yesterday at various times and some two thousand staff in the Palace of Westminster—'

'But only a few would have access to the Not
Content Lobby when the House is sitting,' interrupted
North. 'The only people allowed in either lobby when
the House is in session are the peers, the Badge
Messengers and the clerks.'

'And MPs?' asked Young, a little pointedly.

'Yes,' conceded North. 'A Member of the Commons
is entitled to use both lobbies, perhaps either to meet
a peer or to gain access to the rest of the Lords.
It's a convenient short-cut.'

'To where?' demanded the detective sharply.

'Either to the Sovereign's Entrance, or the Norman
Porch under the Victoria Tower. If it's raining . . .'

'And it was,' murmured the policeman.

'. . . we sometimes walk across the Central Lobby,
into the Peers' Lobby, and along the Not Content
Lobby to avoid making the same journey outside.
Several MPs have their offices in Old Palace Yard off
the Abbey Gardens, which are outside the building
but directly opposite the Lords. It's a popular route
for MPs, and even their staff can use it when the
House isn't sitting. However, the policeman or Doorkeepers at the Peers' Lobby would notice a Member
from the Commons.'

'And does the same route work in reverse? Could
an MP approach the Not Content Lobby from the
other end?'

'Yes, I suppose so,' answered North thoughtfully. 'If
an MP was already in the Lords, having come into
that part of the building from a different access, he
could easily approach the chamber and either of the

two voting lobbies, and then exit through the Peers' Lobby and into the Central Lobby. If he passed through the Peers' Lobby on his way out, he might easily go unnoticed by the Doorkeepers. There are usually two on duty there but they tend to concentrate their attention on people entering the Lords, not leaving it.'

'And just to clear this business of access up once and for all,' concluded Young, 'could an MP approach the Not Content Lobby from the Lords end, if we could call it that, and then exit the same way?'

'I guess so,' confirmed North. 'He might be challenged by a security officer or a Doorkeeper at the Lords end, by the Prince's Chamber, who would have noticed him a few minutes earlier, but I doubt it. There are only four ways in and out of the voting lobbies. Two doorways into the chamber itself, and the main entrances at either end.'

'The trouble is that the Doorkeepers on duty at both ends say that people were passing to and fro all during the relevant period,' said Young. 'All they know for certain is that no unauthorized person was seen in the area. They've made a list of all the people they can recall, but it's a hopeless task . . . It starts at Abercorn and finishes at Zetland. You should see some of these names, St John of Bletso, Mowbray and Stourton, Saye and Sele . . . It's like another era. They even said there had been some youths in. How could that have happened?'

'I forgot another category of people with access to the voting lobbies while the House is sitting,' admitted the MP. 'The eldest sons of peers are allowed to sit on the steps of the Throne during debates. I suppose you would probably regard them as youths.'

Young made a note in his pad and overlooked the MP's comment. 'Do you recall seeing any?'

North cast his mind back to the war crimes debate. 'The chamber was unusually full. I think the average is around three hundred peers visiting the Lords on a normal day, but the debate was an important one. As I recall the Throne steps were quite crowded. There may have been a couple of youngsters.'

'So who else can sit on the Throne steps?' asked Young wearily.

'Apart from the sons of English peers, all Privy Counsellors, retired bishops who have had seats . . . and I think there are a few others. I'll have to check.'

'Ex-bishops? They have access too?'

'They're not ex-bishops. Because there are seats for only twenty-six Lords Spiritual the bishops don't sit for life, unless they've been given a life peerage. They keep their seat until their seventieth birthday, when they lose their see and are replaced by the most senior bishop waiting in the queue. Once they've retired, although they're no longer entitled to a seat in the Lords, they're allowed to perch on the Throne steps. Donnington's over seventy, I think.'

'So that explains his presence in the Not Content Lobby,' said Young. 'He was within his rights to be there.'

'Let's take a look,' said North as he noticed the familiar broad red cover of *Who's Who* on a shelf on the wall behind Young's desk. He reached over and thumbed through the pages. 'Here we are. Donnington, Bishop of. Says here he's, er . . . fifty-five. That doesn't sound right.'

'No,' replied the detective, searching through his notes. 'His proper name's Thresher. William Thresher. That's what he told one of my team last night.'

North leafed through the pages again. 'Yes, he's here. Won the Military Cross in Italy. He's, er, seventy-four.' He paused a moment. 'He lives in Gloucestershire.'

'Then why was he there?' asked Young thoughtfully. 'I wonder.'

'It was a controversial debate,' replied North helpfully. 'The War Crimes Bill is one of those moral issues that the Church feels strongly about. If it's capital punishment, abortion or Sunday trading, the bishops express a view, and invariably vote against the Government. The Church of England is no longer the Tory Party at prayer,' he added a little ruefully.

The allusion was lost on Young who was now clearly preoccupied by the idea that St Oliver's body had been found by a retired prelate with what he evidently regarded as a poor reason for having attended the Lords. 'He could have watched the debate on television. We'll have to establish whether this was a regular afternoon entertainment for the good Bishop, or whether his appearance was unusual. I'm seeing him later this morning and I'd like you to be there.'

'In Gloucestershire?' asked North doubtfully.

Young checked his notes. 'No, he's given his tempor-

ary address in London as care of Lambeth Palace.
Shawcross has fixed for me to see him at midday. If
you can spare the time, it'd be very helpful.'

North grinned his response. Obviously Young wasn't
going to ask twice. 'I'd be delighted. I have one
appointment at eleven-thirty, but if you give me a
moment I'll ask my secretary to postpone it.'

'Good. Cox now. Then I'm due to call on Lady St
Oliver. You may find that interesting too.'

North nodded his head with enthusiasm. 'Does this
mean I'm not a suspect?' he added.

Young continued to make notes in his pad. 'Not
entirely. You were there when the murder occurred.
At the very least you're an important witness. Did
you see anything of interest? And why, incidentally,
were you there? Surely your job is on the other side
of the building?'

For a few moments North pondered the question.
'I was there because I have an interest in the Bill. I
spoke on the Second Reading, and took part in the
Committee stage. It's a fascinating subject and I was
keen to see how the Lords handled it. If they reject
the Bill there'll be a constitutional crisis.'

'Oh really?' muttered Young, clearly uninterested in
the whole subject. 'Who did you see around the time
of the murder?'

'I was standing just inside the chamber, at the Bar
of the House. When I left I spoke briefly to Cox, who
was on duty in the lobby, and he tried to stop me
leaving ... and I saw only one other person there I
knew ... Viktor Strelets.'

'Is he a peer or an MP?'

'Neither. He's a Russian ... The TASS agency correspondent in London. He interviewed me about a month ago concerning the decommissioning of nuclear submarines. I don't think he saw me yesterday, but I spotted him. He's very tall.' North checked a computer printout. 'Yes, he's on the list. He's given a permanent address in Rosary Gardens, SW7.'

'Why would he be in the Lords?'

'Probably to report on the progress of the Bill,' answered the MP. 'The purpose of the Bill is to allow war criminals to be prosecuted in Britain, but the suspects are mainly Russian *émigrés* who came here as refugees. Some are suspected of having committed atrocities against the civilian populations in the Russian territory occupied by the Nazis. When the Soviets demanded their extradition we always refused to hand them over, on the grounds that they would never receive a fair trial in their home country, and that anyway they had become naturalized British subjects.'

'Could Strelets have gained access to the Not Content Lobby?' asked the detective, his interest regained.

'It's unlikely. The police and the Doorkeepers are very wary of strangers wandering around the Palace of Westminster while either House is sitting. If he had been in the East Gallery he might have been able to slip away for a few moments, but I doubt it.'

'What is the East Gallery?'

'The alcove where St Oliver was found is only a few yards from one of the most public areas in the Lords.

It's the staircase that goes up to the Press Room, the Press Gallery and the East Gallery, which is a long corridor running directly above the Not Content Lobby. It gives access to the Strangers' Gallery, the Diplomatic Gallery and the Distinguished Strangers' Gallery.'

'So visitors, journalists and diplomats all share the same staircase up to the gallery,' concluded Young, looking exasperated.

'That's right,' confirmed North, 'but they're all escorted by a Doorkeeper who shows people from the Peers' Lobby, across the Not Content Lobby, and up the stairs.'

'So who else could be there, unescorted?'

'Possibly a journalist from the Press Room. It's a large office shared by all the gallery journalists. They take their notes in the Gallery and then type their reports, or file them to their papers by telephones in the Press Room. So you might expect four or five correspondents in the Gallery and a similar number in the Press Room. They don't need escorts. And,' he added as an afterthought, 'perhaps a peeress from the Earl Marshal's Room.'

'What the hell's that?'

'It's on the principal floor, the same level as the chamber, and is situated directly below the Press Room.'

'Again, very close to the murder?'

'A few yards. It's a writing room reserved for the use of peeresses. Not the wives of peers, but peeresses in their own right.'

'So, this man Strelets was probably within a few feet of the murder, and so were whatever peeresses were in the Earl Marshal's Room?'

'When I saw him, which must have been some minutes afterwards, yes.'

'And wasn't St Oliver a Russian?'

'Not exactly. I think he was a Balt. They hate the Russians.'

'Perhaps the feeling was mutual,' suggested the detective, reaching for a buff file. 'I'll certainly want to talk to him. If you're right, the list of possible suspects has multiplied. What are the other rooms by the East Gallery staircase?'

North considered for a moment before replying. His geography of the Lords was limited. 'The only other room that I can think of is the Moses Room.'

Young checked in his file. 'I have a note here that the Moses Room was unoccupied at the time of the murder. What's it used for?'

'It was built as a court and is called that because it's dominated by a huge painting of Moses carrying the tablets down from the Mount. Now it's only used for large meetings, and the officers of the Lords tend to monopolize it. It's a really magnificent room.'

Clearly Young was not interested in the architectural merits of the Lords. 'I see that it was unlocked, so the killer could have hidden in there immediately after the murder.'

North nodded in agreement. 'There's only one doorway in, as I recall, but it would be easy to hide in there, perhaps behind a desk.'

The detective made a further *aide memoire* to find

out who searched the Moses Room. 'Let's have a word with Mr Cox. He's been waiting long enough.' He picked up the telephone hand-set and spoke briefly to DI Shawcross. Moments later the same officer showed in the black tail-coated Doorkeeper, splendid with his metal buttons, stiff wing-collar and white tie evening dress.

'Please sit down, Mr Cox,' said Young, waving to the chair vacated by North, who had moved to another, larger, leather armchair placed beside the desk. 'I have the statement you gave my colleagues last night regarding the death of Lord St Oliver, and I wanted to give you an opportunity to change it if anything material has occurred to you overnight.'

Cox ran his hand through his thinning grey hair and declined the offer. Although short in stature, he was powerfully built. 'I have nothing to add. The Bishop told me what had happened and I went to see for myself. As soon as I saw His Lordship, or what was left of him, I returned to my post and told Sergeant Kelly. That's all there is to it.'

'Well, let's have a few more details. What time did you start work yesterday?'

'I came in early because I had a party of school-children to show around the Palace. The tour ended at half past twelve, and I then changed into my uniform. Apart from meal breaks, when I am relieved by another Doorkeeper, I stayed at my post, as Door-keeper on the Peers' Lobby throughout the afternoon. Everything was normal until the Bishop came and fetched me.'

'Did you know that he was an ex-bishop?' queried

Young. North winced visibly. The knowledge of the Doorkeepers was unparalleled, but Cox was not offended.

'Of course. We have to know every Member of the Lords and the Commons. But even though he has retired he can still come to the chamber. We see him from time to time. He was terribly shocked... couldn't stop shaking, but he was also quite calm.'

'What happened next?'

'After I told Sergeant Kelly? I asked another messenger, Sam Potter, to go into the chamber and tell Black Rod, and I rang Black Rod's office on my extension. Then I stood by the door to prevent anyone entering or leaving. The only person to do so was Mr North, and I told him I would have to report that he had insisted on leaving. But I can't bar a Member of the Commons from leaving the Lords. I haven't the authority.'

'That's all right,' reassured Young. 'But why did you ring Black Rod's office if you knew he was in the chamber and you had sent Mr Potter to see him?'

'Black Rod is in charge of security in the Lords,' explained the Doorkeeper. 'His staff have contingency plans for all emergencies. Our instructions are to notify Black Rod and his office without delay, whatever the incident.'

'I see. Now, apart from the Bishop did you see anyone in the Not Content Lobby?'

'Not when he called me. Several peers had walked into the lobby earlier in the afternoon, and I have already given the names of those I remembered...

Lord Longford, Lord Annan. I held the doors open for Lord Hailsham ... You should have the list.'

Young nodded to indicate that he had seen it. 'What about visitors? Did any stray into the Not Content Lobby?'

'Impossible,' replied Cox emphatically, as though his professional competence had been questioned.

'You're absolutely certain that none of the tourists in the queue for the gallery could have slipped past you?'

'Definitely. They wait on the benches in the Central Lobby corridor, under the portrait of the trial of Charles the First, until there is room in the gallery, and then we call them from the queue five at a time and direct them to the stairs. There's a Doorkeeper with them all the time.'

'So you were at your post continuously?'

Cox hesitated. 'I went into the chamber a couple of times ... and I saw Mr North standing at the bar.' He nodded at the MP. 'Mr Lawrence was there too, and so was Mr Wheeler. But for the few moments I was inside, Sergeant Kelly was in the lobby immediately outside, together with my colleagues.'

'And how many attendants are usually on duty in the Peers' Lobby?'

'Six Doorkeepers altogether,' corrected Cox, a polite reminder that the Doorkeepers preferred to be called exactly that. 'But yesterday we were one short, and there are probably only two actually in the lobby at any particular moment.'

'And you had no clear view of the entrance to the Not Content Lobby?'

'It's impossible to see through the closed swing doors and around the corner into the voting lobbies.'

The detective paused for a moment, scanning through the rest of Cox's statement. 'Perhaps we can turn to the victim for a moment. Have you any idea who might have wanted to harm St Oliver?' he asked quietly, scarcely looking up from the document in his hands.

'He wasn't well liked, but I couldn't tell you who would have wished him ill. All I can say is that I doubt the murderer came past me.'

'So you think the murderer either approached the Not Content Lobby from the other end or entered directly from the chamber?'

'It sounds odd, doesn't it?' conceded Cox. 'One can't imagine one of Their Lordships doing that to another peer. But I didn't see any oddballs, and nobody went past me.'

Young picked up on his reference to oddballs. 'Who do you mean?'

'The nutters,' replied Cox. 'There are always a few weirdos, the eccentrics—'

'You mean visitors?' interrupted the detective.

'Of course. But they usually concentrate on the Commons. We don't get much trouble in the Lords, and there weren't any kooks yesterday.'

Young made another short notation. 'Tell me a little about yourself. How long have you been a Doorkeeper?'

'Coming up to ten years. I joined from the Royal Marines. Most of the messengers are retired NCOs.'

'And how long were you in the Marines?'

'Twenty-two years. I joined as a lad and I went through Malaya and then saw most of the trouble-spots. Cyprus, Aden and Borneo—'

'The Marines went to Borneo?' broke in North.

'The Special Boat Section did,' replied Cox evenly.

'And did you learn unarmed combat in the SBS?' asked Young casually.

'Of course,' replied Cox.

'And what do you know of Lord St Oliver?'

'Only what I've read in the papers. He was a bit of an old lag.'

'What do you know of him personally?'

'Personally? I suppose I may have handed him the occasional telephone message, but I don't think I've ever addressed a word to him in all the years he's been a Member.'

'And what about before? Did your paths ever cross?'

'If they did, I wasn't aware of it. I don't think he moved in my circles, down Peckham way.'

'And there is nothing else you want to tell me about yesterday?' concluded the policeman.

'That's it, as far as I'm concerned,' said Cox, rising to his feet. 'I hope you catch the loony who did it. I really do.'

After Shawcross had escorted the Doorkeeper out of the room, Young asked North what he thought. 'Clearly Cox has the knowledge to attack a man from behind and cut his throat, but how much skill does it take to surprise an old man and kill him? It sounds to me as though the Bishop is a possibility ... Shocked but calm.'

The detective pushed his chair away from the desk. 'I don't think means is an issue here. If Cox is right, and nobody slipped past without him noticing, then the murderer must have come either from the chamber itself or from the other end of the Not Content Lobby. Tell me, what is at that end?'

'Immediately behind the Throne is a large room called the Prince's Chamber, which only peers can use. Beyond that is the Bishops' Corridor and the Bishops' Bar.'

'The Bishops have their own bar?' queried Young.

'No. The Commons pinched the Pugin Room, which is technically part of the Lords, as a bar to entertain strangers, which left the Lords short of space for their bar. They scrapped the bishops' robing room and turned it into a bar, and the name has stuck.'

'So it rather looks as though our homicidal maniac is also a peer of the Realm ... or a bishop,' said Young with a certain resigned finality.

'Or a journalist ... or a peeress, or perhaps the eldest son of a peer,' murmured North.

Together they walked purposefully across Westminster Hall, the detective apparently oblivious to the magnificence of the surroundings, and pushed through the swing doors at the end into New Palace Yard where an unmarked police saloon was parked on the cobblestones. As North slid into the rear of the Ford, beside the detective, Shawcross climbed into the driver's seat. The car pulled into Parliament Square and Young turned to the MP to continue their conversation, picking up where they had left off.

'Of course, there are other possibilities. Cox himself might have allowed an accomplice into the Not Content Lobby.'

'For the purpose of killing St Oliver?' asked North sceptically. 'For what possible motive? And how would he have known when St Oliver was going to walk into the Not Content Lobby?'

'Perhaps Her Ladyship hired Cox as a hitman,' mused Young, 'but I expect we can think of an even more improbable scenario if we try hard enough.'

'Well, the odds are rather against this being a domestic murder,' observed Shawcross, making his first contribution to the conversation.

'My detective inspector has been making a study of crime profiles,' explained Young. 'His statistics can give you some interesting odds based on thousands of previous cases, mainly in North America.' From Young's tone North could sense that the more experienced officer had little faith in his subordinate's theories.

'And on the basis that no crime is entirely unique?' asked North.

'Something like that,' replied Shawcross as he accelerated past Horse Guards Parade. 'First you take the victim's race, gender and age. That reduces the field. Old men are killed by young men. Sexual orientation and social class are important too. Middle-class white males are killed by C2s – unskilled manual workers.

Old queens are killed by young queens. Serial killers prey on their own ethnic group. Then you take the scene of the crime. Was it home, business, inside or outside?'

'And how do you classify the House of Lords?' asked North.

'Ancient monument,' muttered Young under his breath, as Shawcross admitted he was tempted by office or business. 'It's a public building, of course, but St Oliver sort of worked there. I can't think of many other places with a thousand rooms, two miles of corridors, covering eight acres. As a murder site it's unique, but, leaving that aside, the statistics can tell you quite a lot. Early evening, and what you could term business premises. Finally, there's a weapon and the wounds inflicted. A knife is significant, as is the severity of the wounds and the fact they were concentrated on the neck.'

'And what conclusions have you reached?' asked Young wearily, 'assuming that the woman we are going to meet was his wife in every sense of the word, and her husband was not a closet homosexual.'

'I'm not sure we can make that assumption, but if he was a white heterosexual, and he was killed in a near all-male environment but not for a sexual motive, the field is rather narrow,' replied the younger detective, manoeuvring to overtake a bus.

'I think what Shawcross is trying to say,' added Young with a patently artificial tone of assistance, 'is that none of his statistics are of the slightest help. They don't deal with nobs or the House of Lords. If

St Oliver had been killed anywhere else in England, apart from Buckingham Palace, he could classify this as a probable homosexual incident. If St Oliver had been knifed, poisoned or electrocuted at home, it would have been domestic and we'd be arresting his wife or her lover today, or at least within the week. And if St Oliver had been shot or tied up and burned to death, we'd be looking at his business associates and a possible contract. Maybe an element of Jewish lightning. But the FBI invented this system so my detective inspector is at something of a disadvantage.'

'Take no notice of the Chief Inspector,' retorted Shawcross. 'He's always been uneasy about dealing with Lords since Richard John.'

North was unusually slow on the uptake. 'Richard John? Who he?'

'Richard John Bingham, Earl of—'

'Ah,' said the MP, comprehending. 'Lucan.'

Young grunted and lapsed into silence as his uncharacteristically disrespectful subordinate concentrated on steering the car through the mid-morning traffic of Hyde Park Corner, and North diplomatically changed the subject.

'What do we know about the latest Lady St Oliver?' he enquired. 'By my reckoning she's his fourth wife.'

'I've never met her,' replied Young dismissively. 'I've only just found out that he'd re-married. The last Lady St Oliver I know of married St Oliver six years ago, the widow of a Lancashire landowner. She said she'd stick by her husband when he was convicted and she's never gone on the record about his infidelities.

She's short, dumpy and sixty, and spends most of her time in Preston. Not a very promising murder suspect but the worm may have turned. Anyway, we'll meet the new one in a moment. Let's see what she's like,' he added as Shawcross accelerated up Hill Street and pulled in outside a modern block of flats.

A uniformed porter opened the glass door as they approached and waved the three men towards the lift. 'Fourth floor. Her Ladyship is expecting you,' he said after he had examined Young's warrant card. 'Can't be too careful. The press have been pestering her all morning. No flaming peace, and her being bereaved and all.'

They emerged from the lift. A tall, elegant woman with streaked blonde hair falling across her face stood at the door of a flat across a short lobby. Young stepped forward and introduced himself. 'I'm here to see Lady St Oliver,' he explained. The woman nodded and invited them into a long, L-shaped drawing room. It was bright, lit by the morning sun which emphasized the pastel shades and the colour of the flowers filling two vases. As the three men walked towards a long sofa and armchair, placed opposite a low glass and brass coffee table, North realized that this woman, whom he judged to be in her late thirties, was probably St Oliver's secretary. He was wrong, as became clear when she motioned them to sit down.

'I'm Susan St Oliver,' she said, with a trace of a Yorkshire accent. Leeds, Harrogate or Halifax, thought North. It was refined and subdued, of the kind that was heard at private lunch parties in Ilkley.

Although North knew that the two detectives had been expecting a much older widow, he acknowledged that neither betrayed a hint of surprise. 'You wanted to talk to me about my late husband?' she asked.

'We're very sorry to intrude at such a difficult time,' replied Young evenly. 'As you know, we are conducting a murder inquiry and it is essential that we catch whoever killed Lord St Oliver as soon as possible. Given the circumstances of this terrible crime, Mr North here has kindly agreed to help us . . . He's, er, a Member of Parliament, you know.'

Susan St Oliver flashed a tear-stained smile at North. 'Anything I can do to help,' she said simply. She fidgeted quietly with a gold chain around her waist. To North she was a classic trophy wife, the ambitious, shrewd young newcomer who moves in on an older, richer man. He guessed she had been an airline stewardess, or perhaps an interior decorator or a personal assistant. Nothing as obvious as a masseuse, but still highly manipulative. The kind that caused wills to be rewritten and provoked family feuds.

'How long have you been married to Lord St Oliver?' asked Young. Clearly Young, having been caught unawares by this good-looking young woman, felt he needed to establish some basics. The reliability of the *Daily Mail* as a source had been undermined.

'We were married six week ago, in Venice,' she said. 'I have known Sigi since I first went to work for him, nine years ago in November. He was a wonderful man. No angel, you understand, but a genius. He cut corners in business, as I'm sure you know, but he served his time. He never complained. He was foolish sometimes, but never corrupt. The press could never do anything more than circulate rumours, baseless rumours, and if Sigi had not been to prison he could have sued them all. He was truly a good man.'

Young made no comment. 'Can you tell me when you last saw your husband?'

Lady St Oliver crossed her long, slim legs and brushed her shoulder-length hair away from her face. 'We had breakfast together yesterday morning, and then he worked in his study.' She pointed to a panelled door at the opposite end of the room. 'I left at about eleven, and I knew he had someone coming to see him at eleven-thirty.'

'Do you know who?' asked the detective gently.

'I'm not sure, but I think it was to do with publishing. His appointments diary is on his desk, so you can see for yourself.'

'What sort of publishing was your husband involved with?' asked North.

'He had been offered his own imprint with a large London publisher. He could commission four books a year. It was really a hobby to keep himself busy.'

'And what were his plans after that?' asked Young.

'Most days he had a business lunch, or went to the Lords. He was very involved in this War Crimes Bill, you know. We had intended to go to *Starlight Express* last night, but we cancelled the tickets. He was determined to vote against the Bill.'

'We know he had lunch in the Lords Dining Room

yesterday,' said Young. 'He was in the chamber for Questions, and he attended the war crimes debate. Can you tell me where you went after you left here in the morning?'

'I went to my doctor and then had lunch with a girlfriend at Harvey Nichols.'

'And what time did you come home?' probed Young.

'I suppose I was back by five, five-thirtyish. There was a policeman waiting for me and he told me the dreadful news.'

Young made a note in his pad. 'Perhaps my colleague could take a look at your husband's desk?' he asked. Lady St Oliver nodded, and, without prompting, Shawcross strode across the room and disappeared into the study. 'Can you think of anyone who would have wished your husband harm?' continued Young.

She tossed her hair and smiled again. 'Plenty. Sigi had made lots of enemies, here and elsewhere. But it didn't amount to much and he thrived on confrontation. I can't think of any single person who would have wanted to go so far as to kill him. Ruin him financially, yes. Murder, no.'

'What about threats? Strange telephone calls, hang-ups?'

'None,' she said firmly.

'What about his former wives?' probed Young. 'Was there any bitterness there?'

'Sigi and I rarely spoke about them,' she replied. 'They were history.'

'You say plenty of people wished him ill,' pressed

the detective. 'That's unusual. To what do you attribute that?'

'Over the years Sigi has lost and made several fortunes. Some of his partners have been greedy. Others are jealous of his success. Everybody has an opinion about Sigi. He's not one of those neutral, grey men.' North noted that she had slipped into what was evidently her natural Yorkshire dialect, and was talking about her dead husband in the present tense. 'Lots wanted to do him down, but none had the guts to really face him.'

'And these individuals who wanted him ruined. Are they figures from the distant past, or linked to his present business activities?'

'Probably both, I should think. Sigi has been around a long time. As they say, he knows where the bodies are buried. He was angry that no one had spoken up for him at his trial. All the people he had enriched, all the politicians to whom he had made contributions. They turned on him, and Sigi boasted a long memory. His latest publishing venture was going to make him another fortune. He was going to expose the lot of them,' she asserted with enthusiasm.

The detective considered what he had heard for a few moments. 'Are you saying that Lord St Oliver was going to publish revelations about dealings with his former, er, colleagues?' Young's antennae sensed a whiff of blackmail.

'He didn't discuss his plans with me in detail,' said the widow, backtracking perceptibly. 'He had signed up a few interesting authors. His favourite expression was that he was going to rattle a few cages.'

'Do you know who any of these authors were?' queried Young.

'Jonathan Aldworth was one. He was also looking for someone to do the inside story of the *Himmler Diaries*.' North raised an eyebrow. He had watched the young Viscount Aldworth take his place in the House yesterday after Lord Tremaine's conciliatory speech. A few candid disclosures from Aldworth would really set the cat among the pigeons. His galère consisted of the daughters of cabinet ministers and the dope-peddling sons of celebrities. Just the news of such a book would send pulses racing in the tabloids and cause palpitations in some of the country's oldest stately homes. As for the notorious *Himmler Diaries*, the ill-fated venture that had brought down St Oliver's last publishing company, he wondered why the peer would have wanted to relive the agonies of what had turned out to be an embarrassing and expensive hoax. Unwisely, in return for a large fee from Sigi, Staveley had authenticated the forged documents and thereby had not only compromised his integrity but had destroyed a lifetime of academic endeavour. When the diaries were exposed as fakes fabricated in Hamburg by a well-known hoaxer Staveley had immediately become the subject of ridicule and his reputation had been shredded. The news footage of Staveley's press conference, at which Sigi had announced what had been hailed by his publicity staff as the publishing triumph of the decade, was now as well-known as the infamous appearance of Michael

Fish, the BBC weatherman who had ridiculed reports of a hurricane hours before much of the south of England had been devastated by the worst weather of the century. North could see that just these two projects alone could cause serious trouble, but the point appeared to have been lost on the detective who dropped the issue and moved on.

'What can you tell me about your relationship with Lord St Oliver? I'm sorry to pry, but I have to ask,' said Young.

'I'm pregnant,' she said simply. 'Doesn't that speak for itself?' There was an awkward pause while North considered a few inappropriate questions he would have liked to ask concerning the baby's father. Judging from her trim figure, she could not be very far gone. 'Sigi had always wanted children,' she continued, 'but Maisie never had any. He was so excited at the prospect of becoming a father, even though he had left it so late.'

'And speaking of the last Lady St Oliver,' interjected Young, 'what did she think of your marriage?'

'Like I said, we rarely discussed Sigi's former wives. But Maisie never seemed resentful. The divorce went through in December and I have not heard from her since.' North exchanged a glance with the detective who gave him a slight nod. It was a sign that he was free to intervene.

'As I recall, neither the divorce nor your marriage was reported in the newspapers. Is that right?' asked the MP.

'I really don't know,' replied Lady St Oliver. 'We

were on a cruise in the Pacific when the divorce became absolute so I didn't read the papers. And our marriage in Venice was a very private affair. That's how Sigi wanted it. Private and romantic. We went off by boat to Torcello and then had a wedding breakfast at Harry's Bar. Who could have wanted more?'

'And are you a Catholic?' asked North quietly. Lady St Oliver looked unsure of herself, for the first time, and momentarily dropped her mask. But she recovered swiftly and rose to her feet. 'My religion is entirely my own affair,' she said imperiously. 'And if you'll excuse me, I really need some rest.'

Young was startled by her sudden move but was conciliatory. 'We much appreciate your time, Lady St Oliver. We'll be in touch again when we have some news to report. My colleague will return the items he removes from Lord St Oliver's desk, and in the meantime I must ask that the study remains sealed. I'll also have an officer placed on your door to ensure you are left in peace.'

Susan St Oliver gave the Detective Chief Inspector a short and artificial smile. 'If you think that necessary, I'm very grateful. Perhaps just until this is all cleared up?'

'That's right, madam,' responded the policeman. 'I don't want you pestered by the media. You deserve some rest.' Young and North moved towards the front door, where they were joined by Shawcross, who carried under his arm a large leather desk diary and some buff cardboard files. As Lady St Oliver opened the door, Young turned to shake her hand. 'One final thing... In case we have to get in touch with your husband's solicitors, do you know who they are?'

'David Simons, of Simons & Simons, in the City,' she replied without a moment's hesitation. For someone who knew so little about her late husband's business, thought North, she certainly had no difficulty in remembering the name of his lawyer.

The thought had occurred to DCI Young, as they took the lift down to the ground floor. 'St Oliver was a life peer, wasn't he? So there's no title to inherit.'

'No,' said North. 'But Susie's son will be an honourable.' As North said it, he realized it didn't sound quite right.

Chapter Three

The Viscount

As Shawcross pulled out into the traffic clogging Hill Street the detective turned on North. 'What the hell was all that religious nonsense? We were doing fine until you barged in. She's right. Her religious opinions are nothing to do with this investigation and we need her co-operation. I thought you were going to make some helpful point, not give a newly bereaved widow a reason to complain about police harassment.'

'Sigi St Oliver was a Jew. The only church on Torcello is a very ancient Catholic one. I merely asked her about the apparent contradiction.'

Young was silent for a few moments. 'How do you know about the religious denomination of churches in Venice? Made a study of them?' he asked sarcastically.

'There's only one church on Torcello, which is a tiny island ... quite a long boat trip from Venice. It's a day out, and there's a wonderful restaurant on the island too. But a Jew marrying a Yorkshire lass there? It's improbable.'

'So are you saying that she's lying about her marriage?' demanded Young, somewhat chastened.

'Not necessarily. But it's odd.'

'But nothing to do with the murder inquiry,' rejoined the detective who leaned towards his subordinate. 'Anything in the study?'

'There were two locked drawers in his desk, and some files on the top. I've taken what was there, including some bank statements and his appointments book.'

'Anything in it for eleven-thirty yesterday?'

'Just the initials "JA". Some telephone numbers written in the margin, and a line through the word "Starlight" at eight o'clock.'

'OK,' acknowledged Young. 'Ask the Incident Room to empty the desk and seal the study. Then ask West End Central to put a man on the door. Nothing to leave the flat without my written authorization. Do it now.'

Shawcross leaned across and removed a radio handset from the glove compartment. 'Lambeth Palace next, chief?' he asked as the car approached Park Lane.

'Yes,' said Young, leaning back in his seat. 'The good Bishop is next. Now, apart from suspecting Lady St Oliver's commitment to Catholicism, what other conclusions did you draw?' He was addressing North.

'A cut above the office bimbo,' replied North, as Shawcross spoke quietly into the radio microphone, 'and she fits into His Lordship's comfortable Mayfair pad very easily. But if I was the previous Lady St Oliver I probably wouldn't have been as sanguine about my husband's mistress as Susan suggests she was.'

'Perhaps Maisie had had enough of Sigi,' countered Young. 'Was pleased to be shot of the old crook.'

'Maybe,' replied North. 'But she took her time about it, didn't she? They must have been married for quite a while. It rather reminds me of a conversation between Sir Alec Douglas Home, when he was Ted Heath's foreign secretary, and the Pope. Sir Alec was pushed for something to say in a lull in the proceedings, and he speculated about how history might have been different if Khrushchev had been assassinated instead of Jack Kennedy. Apparently the Pope thought for a couple of moments and then whispered, "I'll bet Aristotle Onassis wouldn't have married Mrs Khrushchev."'

Young murmured something incomprehensible, and then more audibly added, 'We'll have to see the other Lady St Oliver. The Incident Room can trace her. This viscount, too. What do you know about him?' he asked the MP.

'He's Viscount Aldworth . . . Eldest son of the Earl of Manston. I think you'll find quite a few drug convictions in criminal records, including a spell in the Scrubs for attempted theft. He became addicted to morphine after an appalling car smash when he was up at university. He never fully recovered and was in tremendous pain for years. I think he's kicked it now, after several rehabilitation programmes. Unlike the John Jermyns and Jamie Blandfords, who inherited plenty of money to support their habits, Jonti's father never really had any cash. Expensive children, but no readies. He was a Cabinet minister in Macmillan's government and sat in the Lords. As the eldest son of an earl, Jonti can sit on the steps of the Throne, but he has to wait until his father dies before he can take his seat. But as I said, there're no family estates to inherit. This is churchmice territory.'

'Lord Manston was in the Cabinet and in the Lords simultaneously, and his son's called Aldworth?'

'Every department of government has to have a spokesman in the Lords. Sometimes, like Peter Carrington or David Young, they make the Cabinet. The Leader of the Lords is automatically a member of the Lords. Even the Prime Minister can be in the Lords. As for Jonti, Aldworth is a courtesy title belonging to his father. I don't recall what their family name is.'

There was a moment's pause while the detective mulled over what he had been told. 'Aldworth's Christian name is Jonathan, eh?' asked Young.

'Yes, that's right,' he replied, and then, 'You're right!' he exclaimed. 'He could be the JA in St Oliver's diary.'

'And what has the Viscount Aldworth got to offer as a contribution to the nation's literature?' queried Young.

'My guess is a book entitled *My Life of Drugs among the Toffs*. If he was to spill the beans about his contemporaries he would do more than cause a few red faces. Remember that girl who died of an overdose at an Oxford party? Aldworth gave evidence at the inquest and said he couldn't remember who else had been at the party or who had supplied the drugs. Suppose his memory improved?'

Young rubbed his chin thoughtfully. 'So Aldworth could lift the lid on his society pals. But that would make *him* a target, not his publisher.'

North conceded the point. 'Getting rid of Sigi won't have stopped Aldworth if he thinks this is a scheme to make some money. He'll simply find another publisher and I don't suppose he'd have far to look.'

'So in terms of suspects,' said the detective, 'we've not much to go on. The wife – if that is what she is – doesn't look promising, and the prospective author is short of a motive.'

'If you think about it,' agreed North, 'Sigi's death is against Aldworth's interests. On the basis that he's been paid on advance, he wouldn't normally receive any more money until the book had been delivered and then published. With Sigi gone, he may have to wait longer to see the book released and his first royalty cheque.'

Shawcross accelerated the Ford away from the traffic lights at Hyde Park Corner and headed towards Victoria. He deftly manoeuvred through the traffic and swung the car into Vauxhall Bridge Road, heading south towards the river.

'Did you see Aldworth in the chamber yesterday?' asked Young.

'He was there, all right,' confirmed North, recalling the tall, lanky young man with the mop of unkempt hair, always a contrast to the stooped figures of the other peers sitting alongside him. 'He's Jewish, so he's likely to have been interested in the debate, even if he was the wrong generation.'

Young leaned forward to Shawcross and tapped him on the shoulder. 'Another message for the Incident Room. Find Lord Aldworth and arrange for me to see him this afternoon at three.' The subordinate nodded that he had understood and relayed the request over the radio as the car accelerated along the south bank of the Thames, past the Scotland Yard annexe at Tintagel House, which accommodated some of the CID's most sensitive branches. Moments later they were parking at the entrance to Lambeth Palace. A gatekeeper showed them into a sparsely furnished sitting room which more resembled a dentist's waiting room. 'I'll tell His Lordship you're here,' he said as he closed the door. The two detectives settled into armchairs while North examined a wall of photographs portraying the Archbishop of Canterbury being received by various foreign dignitaries. From a bookshelf he selected a current copy of *Crockford's*, the ecclesiastical directory. Then the door swung open and a tall, white-haired man with ruddy cheeks and bushy eyebrows entered. For a man of seventy-four who had a sedentary existence, noted North, the Bishop of Donnington looked very fit.

'Good morning ... Or is it good afternoon, gentlemen? I'm sorry for keeping you waiting. This is a really dreadful business and I'm still not over the shock of it. Poor St Oliver.'

After Young had made the introductions, he explained the purpose of his visit. 'I have a copy of the statement you made yesterday evening to one of my colleagues, and I wondered if there was anything that had occurred to you since then that you wanted to add?'

The Bishop appeared puzzled. 'I'm afraid you'll have to speak up. I'm rather deaf nowadays.'

The detective repeated the question.

'I told the officer everything I could remember,' said the Bishop. 'I was walking through the Not Content Lobby and I saw a leg protruding from under the red velvet drape hanging across the lobby door into the chamber. When I drew it to one side I found poor old St Oliver. He was a ghastly sight. I instantly went to fetch the police.'

'And between the moment when you found the body and when you reached the Lords' Lobby, you saw no one else?'

'Not that I recall,' replied the Bishop uncertainly. 'I was in rather a state, but I certainly spoke to no one until I reached the Doorkeeper.'

'Can you tell me how well you knew St Oliver?' asked Young.

'Hardly at all, personally,' said the cleric. 'Naturally I had read about him in the newspapers, and he was fairly notorious in the Lords because of his past, but he'd done good work on the Penal Affairs Group. I don't think I ever spoke to him.'

'You never had any business dealings with him, or anything of that kind?'

'Heavens, no,' sniffed the older man, the colour rising in his cheeks.

'And you came up to London from Gloucestershire specifically for this debate?'

'Oh yes. Now that I've retired I am disqualified from speaking in the Lords, so I was relying upon others to oppose the Bill last evening, but because of all this I was unable to listen to the rest of the debate.'

'So it was entirely coincidental that you encountered St Oliver. You had not intended to have a word with him, or discuss the debate with him?'

'Absolutely not. As I say, I didn't know the man.' North judged that the increasing brevity of the Bishop's replies matched his diminishing patience.

The change in tone had also registered with the detective, who adopted a different tack. 'You retired from the Lords four years ago?'

'Yes. The Lords Spiritual retire at seventy,' explained Donnington, 'to make way for younger men. All the bishops from the other sees are eligible, except, as I recall, for the Bishop of Sodor and Man, who has a seat automatically in the House of Keys on the Isle of Man, and the Bishop of Gibraltar in Europe, a diocese which was created only quite recently—'

'Is there nothing you can say that might shed some light on this incident?' interrupted the DCI, clearly uninterested in how bishops came to sit in the Upper House.

'If there was anything I could think of, I'd tell you right away,' he assured the detective. 'I've thought about little else during the night, but I am afraid I cannot be of much help to you. Clearly there is a very troubled soul at large, but I have no idea who is responsible for this tragedy.'

'Thank you for your thoughts, anyway. Perhaps you could tell me a little about your own background. It's purely routine. I see from your entry in *Who's Who* that you were a gunner and served in Italy.'

'That's right. North Africa, Sicily and Italy. That's why I'm so hard of hearing. I found my vocation and joined the Church after the war.'

'And you now live in Gloucestershire?'

'My wife and I have a small cottage near Stroud. She is very crippled by arthritis so she stays in the country on the rare occasions I come up to London.'

'And you usually stay here?' Young gestured to the surroundings of Lambeth Palace.

'The Archbishop is a very old friend. We spent three years together on the World Council of Churches and he offers me a bed if one's free when I'm up in town.'

Young glanced at North. 'I think that's nearly everything . . . But perhaps Mr North has something.' It was as much a question to the MP.

'I understand that you're still the honorary chaplain to the Baltic community in London,' said North. 'Is that right?'

'What? Oh, yes,' said the Bishop, evidently surprised. 'It's purely a nominal role nowadays but I attend divine service a couple of times a year at the Baltic church. I've really retired now.'

'And how did you acquire this, er, Baltic connection?' North could see that the interest of the detectives had been regained. Both had re-opened their notebooks.

'After the war I was stationed in Bremen, in the British zone of occupation. There were several big DP camps under our administration and that was where I came into contact with the refugees from Latvia and Estonia. When they eventually settled in England I was invited to become chaplain to their congregation.'

'And did you know St Oliver was of Lithuanian origin?' asked North quietly.

'Yes, I did,' replied the Bishop. 'He was not prominent in the expatriate community, but I certainly knew of him. Though, as I said before, I never actually met him. I don't think he mixed at all with other Lithuanians.'

'Do you know why?' asked Young. 'Isn't that rather unusual?'

'Not all the refugees from Eastern Europe are interested in maintaining their links with the old country. Some are completely assimilated into the host community and prefer to forget painful memories.'

'And did St Oliver have painful memories?' asked North.

The Bishop adjusted the hearing aid nestling discreetly in his ear. 'I never spoke to him so I don't know,' he answered with a trace of irritation.

'You may not have spoken to him,' conceded Young, 'but what was the view taken of him by other Lithuanians?'

'I don't think he was particularly liked, but that's only an impression I gained. St Oliver was not a Christian so his popularity was never a subject that

I remember ever being discussed.' As an afterthought he added, 'I can't think why the Garter King of Arms allowed him to take that preposterous title. He was neither a Christian nor a saint. It's really insulting.'

The DCI ignored the observation and, at a nod from the detective, North tried a longshot. 'Do you know Viktor Strelets?'

The Bishop suddenly looked up, as though he had received an unexpected electric shock. 'Indeed. He's a Soviet journalist.'

'When was the last time you saw him?' asked the detective.

The Bishop looked confused, and his hand rubbed his bushy eyebrows. 'I haven't seen Viktor for a couple of years, I'm sure. Why do you want to know?'

'It's just routine,' smiled Young reassuringly. 'But you definitely didn't see him yesterday?'

'Good heavens, no,' said the Bishop. 'Was he at the Lords?'

'He was taking a close interest in the war crimes debate, from the Press Gallery. Can you think why?' asked the detective.

'It's a very controversial subject,' explained the Bishop, 'and I can well imagine his interest. Among those accused of war crimes by Moscow are several people from the Baltic. I think they're mainly Estonians and Byelorussians who were inducted into the SS during the war, but the Russians and the Ukrainians have long memories. Now they have British nationality and have been protected from extradition to Moscow. The Russians publish lists of suspects from

time to time, but the expatriate community is quite
determined to resist the pressure. Many of those
names are well known anti-Communists who would
be executed by the regime for political reasons the
moment they landed in Russia.'

'So Strelets sees this legislation as a way of persecu-
ting Moscow's political opponents?' asked Young.

'Maybe. But Strelets would certainly want to report
on the passage of the Bill. It would be very news-
worthy in the Soviet Union. It might even signal a
change in British policy. At present there is no extradition between the two countries.'

'There's no extradition for war criminals, or for
those accused of political offences?' queried Young.

'Neither,' said the Bishop. 'At least a dozen of those
on the Moscow lists have been sentenced to death in
their absence. The Government's policy has always
been that it will not extradite British or any other
citizens to face capital punishment abroad. That has
been the stalemate that has existed since the Nurem-
berg trials, and rightly so in my judgement.'

'And what will this legislation change?' asked the
detective, now convinced that the proceedings of the
Lords may, after all, have had a bearing on the
murder of Lord St Oliver.

'The Bill allows British citizens to be tried in
England for crimes they committed overseas, before
they acquired British nationality,' said the Bishop
simply.

'But you are opposed to it,' added Young.

'I think there has been enough suffering already

and we must draw a line across the past. I also share some of the reservations about evidence which have concerned the lawyers. How can you rely on eye-witness testimony when we are dealing with events of more than forty years ago?'

'But if your family had been butchered by the Nazis,' countered North, 'you might feel rather differently.'

'Of course I respect the views of the Jewish community,' acknowledged the Bishop. 'They have suffered unspeakably and they have a right to be bitter. But some want vengeance, which I could not condone.'

'And how well do you know Strelets?' asked Young. 'I notice that you called him Viktor.'

'Don't be fooled by his cosmopolitan appearance, or his sophisticated airs,' warned the Bishop. 'The man is a hardliner. He reminds me of the men we saw in Germany after the war, the Smersh agents who scoured the camps for the Russians who had fought against Stalin. They were utterly ruthless, completely committed to a policy of liquidating the enemies of Communism. None of the poor devils whom they seized from the camps survived. And we were powerless to intervene. Our instructions were to allow the Russian officials access to our prisoners. Sometimes we even heard the crackle of machine-gun fire from the Soviet zone.'

'But surely Smersh only existed in the James Bond books,' protested North.

'Smersh existed, I promise you,' said the Bishop. 'The officers may have had the green shoulderboards of the NKVD but the men we saw were executioners. Smersh is Russian for "death to spies". Under the rules of the Control Commission, they were entitled to repatriate all Soviet prisoners. That meant a bullet in the back of the head for the men who had fought with Vlassov's army, and their families.'

'I think we have taken up enough of your time, Bishop,' announced Young, bringing the interview to a close. 'If anything else occurs to you, perhaps you would be kind enough to let me know. Here's my card, and this is the Incident Room number.' The detective scrawled the direct line telephone number on the back of the card. The Bishop accepted it and escorted his three visitors to their car.

'Back to the Commons, and then the Incident Room,' instructed Young as Shawcross started the engine and signalled the communications centre his callsign.

'And where the fuck did you get all this Baltic chaplain stuff?' demanded Young, as the car edged into the traffic at Lambeth roundabout. 'Don't pull a stroke on me like that again. If you have information you must share it with me.'

'I'm sorry,' apologized North. 'But there was no time. I only spotted Donnington's other role when I looked him up in *Crockford's*.'

'And what the fuck is *Crockford's*?' said the detective.

'It's a kind of ecclesiastical yearbook. There was a copy in the room where we saw the bishop. I was reading his entry as he came in, and I didn't have time to point it out to you.'

Young accepted the explanation with poor grace, and changed the subject. 'The Bishop was evasive about St Oliver. I think he knew him before the murder, and there's something going on between this TASS fellow, Strelets, and the Bishop.'

North had reached the same conclusion. 'St Oliver is a Lithuanian and comes to this country after the war as a refugee, Donnington is involved in the running of refugee camps for Lithuanians, and Strelets turns up, taking an interest in war criminals from the Baltic countries. Hardly a coincidence.'

'But St Oliver could hardly have been a war criminal on the run from the Soviets,' countered Young. 'He was a Jew . . . a victim.'

'What is rather odd,' pondered North, 'is that Susan St Oliver told us that her husband had *opposed* the War Crimes Bill. And yet, as you say, he was Jewish. If she was right, then he was probably in a minority of one. On such an emotive issue, how could he oppose the legislation? It doesn't make sense.'

They were interrupted by the ring of the phone. Shawcross said over his shoulder, 'I've got the Incident Room. Lord Aldworth's at his home, in Cheyne Walk. Do you want to see him right away?'

'Tell them we'll go straight there,' said the senior detective, noting North's nod of approval. 'We'll forget lunch and grab a sandwich later. And let's call in Strelets. Tell the Incident Room to pick him up this afternoon. I'll see him at three.'

Shawcross relayed the message and moved into the next line of traffic to turn west on to the Embankment. 'Let's consider collusion for a moment,' said

Young. 'Might Donnington and Strelets conspire together to kill St Oliver?'

'What's the motive?' queried the MP. 'Strelets is at the very least a Communist, if not KGB. Presumably he wants the regime's enemies shipped home to face a firing squad. If St Oliver wasn't a wanted war criminal, the Soviets must have regarded him as a political opponent. But Strelets' interests don't coincide with what we know about the Bishop. He sounds pretty anti-Communist to me, and he says he's against the War Crimes Bill because he wants to forget the past. Their views diverge, not converge.'

'I think we need to know much more about St Oliver's politics,' said Young. 'Was he an anti-Communist, and did his name ever appear on any list of war criminals published by the Soviets? We need the Branch. This is really their field. Political activity by *émigrés* is exactly the kind of data they collect.' He tapped Shawcross on the shoulder. 'When we get back, can you ask for a briefing from them on St Oliver and Strelets? Or, better still, use a landline while we see Aldworth.'

'I don't think St Oliver was ever considered anti-Communist,' remarked North. 'Most of Wilson's cronies were thought to be a sight too close to the Kremlin. Rudi Sternberg and his ilk. Now he's Lord Plurendon. He made his fortune from trading with Moscow, and he wasn't alone. There were half a dozen others in Wilson's resignation honours.' The car sped along the Embankment, was delayed for a few moments at the usual bottleneck at Chelsea Bridge, and then turned up Tite Street, heading for the Royal Hospital Road.

'This Aldworth is a good suspect, in your estimation?' asked Young. 'A dope fiend, a convicted felon and what else?'

'A reformed chemical abuser is the politically correct term,' replied the MP easily. 'He's made quite a reputation speaking about addiction problems and is involved in several rehabilitation schemes. He's well liked in the Lords. I think he's given up the nose candy.'

'What's his job?'

'No job. He's unemployable.'

'His links with St Oliver are simply to generate cash?'

'Probably. He's never had any money and after his car accident he wasn't fit enough to work.'

'So what's he doing in Cheyne Walk?' demanded the detective.

North shrugged his shoulders. The terrace overlooking the Thames was one of the most sought after addresses in London. The residents included Mick Jagger, Paul Getty Jnr, Jane Asher and Ken Follett. 'The Incident Room says his address is the basement flat at number fifteen,' interrupted Shawcross. 'Do you want a Criminal Records Office check before we arrive?'

'Always handy,' agreed Young. 'Have you a date of birth?' he asked the MP.

'He's probably ten years younger than me, so that'd make him born in about 1961. The exact date will be in *Debrett's* or *Burke's.*' Moments later the radio crackled with the car's callsign and Shawcross switched up the volume so his two passengers could hear the despatcher read the message.

'Aldworth, Alpha, Lima, Delta, Whisky, Oscar, Romeo, Tango, Hotel. Jonathan Charles. Born 8 November 1962. Two convictions theft. Two class A possession. Disqualified until September. No warrants outstanding.'

'Yeah, received, Delta Echo,' replied Shawcross as he approached the junction of Chelsea Manor Street. They drew up outside the ornate wrought-iron gates of a magnificent, large, double-fronted, five-storey house. 'Basement flat, guv. I'll find a landline and be back in a couple of minutes.' The two men stepped out of the car and walked through the gate, the family crest of Lord Godolphin dominating the railings. Set in the brickwork above the balcony were reliefs of some famous former Chelsea residents, including Thomas More. The site had once been part of a country estate which had stretched from Chelsea Manor down to the river.

They traversed the paved front garden and descended a short flight of steps. As they approached the front door, a younger man stepped forward from the entrance. He was wearing cords and a polo-neck sweater, and walked with a limp. His hair was lank and unwashed, and the hinge of his spectacles was held together with tape.

'Hello, Chief Inspector. I'm Jonti Aldworth.' He gave North a smile of recognition. 'Hi, Phil. Are you a suspect too? Do come in.'

They stepped down two more steps, into a dimly lit sitting room. A wicker seat and a banquette under the double windows, or a large cushion on the floor, were the only places to sit.

'We're here to talk to you about the death of Lord St Oliver yesterday afternoon,' opened Young. 'I have a colleague who will be joining us shortly, and I propose to give you a caution . . .'

'Don't bother,' replied the peer, running his hand through his long curls. 'I'm quite familiar with police procedure. I don't need a lawyer and I'm perfectly happy to help in any way I can.'

'Very well,' said the chief inspector. 'I understand that you had a meeting with Lord St Oliver yesterday morning?'

'That's correct,' said Aldworth. 'I had an appointment to see him at his flat in Hill Street. I left at around twelve-thirty.'

'Did you go to the Lords?'

'I did, but not until later. I had lunch first at Harry's Bar.'

'Who with?'

'The Duchess of York and a couple of other friends.'

The detective seemed nonplussed. 'Who were the others?'

'Kim Smith-Bingham, Kate Fletcher . . . They'll confirm that.'

The detective made a note of the names but gave no indication of surprise. If Aldworth had intended to introduce Fergie's name to impress the policeman, he had failed. 'What time did you reach the Lords?'

'I caught a cab at around three, I suppose.'

'What was the purpose of your meeting with St Oliver?'

'My book.'

'The one you've agreed to write for St Oliver?'

'Yes. It's a sort of autobiography mixed with a few Taki-style anecdotes.'

'And when is it to be released?'

'I don't know. Sigi never told me. I gave him the manuscript yesterday and he was going to tell me when the editors had finished cutting out the libel.'

'And you left on good terms?'

'Of course.'

'And you saw him in the Lords yesterday afternoon?'

'I saw him in the chamber, but we didn't speak.' Aldworth settled back and offered a cigarette, which was refused by both visitors.

'Did you leave the chamber at any time during the debate?' continued the detective.

'I may have slipped out for a jimmy riddle, but only for a moment.' The doorbell rang, prompting Aldworth to break off and open it. Detective Inspector Shawcross entered and took a seat beside North on the banquette. Aldworth drew heavily on his Marlboro and continued. 'I only heard about the murder during Tony Tremaine's speech. It was then that I had to give my name to one of the policemen. Then another policeman called about an hour ago, and here you are. That's all I know.'

'Take me through what happened yesterday morning,' said Young. 'What time did you arrive at Hill Street?'

'About eleven thirty, eleven forty-five. I don't remember exactly.'

'And then?'

'Sigi opened the door and we sat in his drawing room.'

'Did you see Lady St Oliver?'

'No.'

'Did you see anyone else?'

'In the flat? No. I think there was a doorman on duty downstairs; I don't recall.'

'And what happened next?'

'Well, I handed over the manuscript and that was it.'

'But you stayed for three-quarters of an hour,' pointed out Young.

'Well, we had to discuss some financial details. That took a little time.'

'What sort of details?'

'That's private,' asserted Aldworth.

'It is not,' answered the detective swiftly. 'This is a murder investigation and you were one of the last people to see Lord St Oliver alive. If you don't give me your full co-operation I will have you charged with obstruction. This is not an idle threat. Do I make myself clear?'

Aldworth nodded uncertainly. 'My contract gives me a payment upon delivery of the manuscript, and another on publication. I asked for my cheque and Sigi said I'd have to wait. That wasn't part of the deal. So we talked about money a little.'

'So you argued about money?' corrected Young.

'Not exactly. Sigi's very sharp. I just didn't want to

be another scalp on his belt. He only respects people who are firm with him. I knew that the contract stipulated a payment upon completion of the book, and he was quibbling. We compromised by him agreeing to pay me as soon as he had read it. We parted the best of friends.'

'How long have you had a business relationship with St Oliver?'

'I first met him in the Lords two years ago. We were on a committee together and he suggested that others might benefit from my experiences. He invited me to lunch, at Les Ambassadeurs, and I agreed to write a book for him. I wasn't surprised that he tried to shortchange me . . . I'd been warned.'

'Oh really . . . who by?' enquired the detective.

'Tony Rendell.'

'Is that Lord Rendell?'

'Yeah,' said Aldworth casually. 'He said that Sigi had cheated him out of a fortune, so I suppose I should have known that Sigi'd try it on.'

Young thought he recalled seeing Lord Rendell's name on the list of peers who had attended the Lords during the war crimes debate. He made a note to check, remembering his name being linked to a call-girl scandal, and then continued the interview. 'The press say the book is going to be a sensation, full of embarrassing revelations. Is that right?'

'That's total crap,' retorted Aldworth. 'Because I've got a record the press can write what they like about me. Most of it is sheer rubbish.'

'Perhaps I can be the judge of that,' replied the

detective. 'May I see the manuscript?'

'Sigi has it,' said the younger man. 'He was going to Xerox it and let me have a copy.'

'So there's only one copy and you gave it to St Oliver yesterday morning?' North caught Young glance at Shawcross, who almost imperceptibly shook his head.

'That's right,' confirmed Aldworth, who seemed not to have noticed the exchange of looks between the detectives. 'And don't look so worried, Phil. You're not in it.'

'How well did you know St Oliver?' continued Young, ignoring the peer's aside to North.

'Hardly at all. I went to a couple of his parties, and I suppose we had about three or four meetings to discuss how the book was getting along. Apart from that, I occasionally saw him in the Lords, but that's all. We weren't bosom buddies.'

'But you didn't dislike him?' queried Young.

'He was OK. Like I say, tightfisted when it came to money, but OK. He started to drink his own bathwater . . . You know, believe his own press. I quite enjoyed him really. He was always telling me amazing stories about his past.'

'Such as?' prompted the detective.

'Oh, I don't know . . . He told me once that he had been asked to put in an offer to build a home for the corrupt leader of some Labour council up north and had put in a bid of zero. When he didn't get the work he made an appointment to see the councillor to ask why he hadn't got the job. The councillor told Sigi that he had been the overbidder by £10,000!'

'Did he confide in you about his business?'

'Not really. He wanted to rebuild his publishing empire and he needed authors. Hence the parties, hence me. All Sigi was interested in was making a splash and thumbing his nose to the establishment. Nothing else really mattered.'

'And what about Lady St Oliver?'

'Susie? I don't think they ever married. She uses the title for convenience, but Sigi was too smart to marry her. What a bow-wow.'

'Are you sure they weren't married?'

'Not one hundred per cent, but it would have been out of character for him. After the end of his third marriage his favourite motto was "If it floats, flies or fucks, rent it." '

Young had reached the end of his questions. 'I'll want you to come into the station this afternoon and make a statement. Can you come at four?'

'Why should I make a statement? I've done nothing wrong and I've told you all I know.'

'It's just routine,' replied the detective.

'I've heard that before,' said Aldworth. 'You'll tip off the press and by the evening news I'll have become a murder suspect.'

'You *are* a murder suspect,' retorted the detective. 'None of my officers will leak news of your statement, but if you don't agree to come I'll have you arrested.' He looked around the flat. 'We could also issue a search warrant. The choice is yours.'

The threat had reached its intended target. 'Don't sweat. I'll come.'

'Is this your flat?' asked the detective.

'It's borrowed. It belongs to the old bat who lives upstairs. I'm sort of house-sitting while her tenant is away.'

'Very well,' said Young, as he headed for the door. 'And, incidentally, I think you ought to stay in London, at least for the time being.'

Once out in the street, out of earshot of the viscount, Shawcross confided to Young that he had spoken to the Branch. 'They want to see you, at the Yard.'

Young considered this development for a moment. 'What about Strelets?'

'The Deputy Assistant Commissioner mentioned him to me. I said we intended to pull him in this afternoon, but he suggested we delay that. So I took the liberty of cancelling the Incident Room's pick-up request.'

'You spoke to the DAC?' observed Young.

'I asked for the duty officer but when I mentioned St Oliver I was put through to Phelan. Took me a bit by surprise as well.'

'Fine,' murmured Young. To have his DI conversing with the head of the Special Branch was quite a novelty, thought the older detective. Evidently St Oliver was not of mere passing interest to the Branch. For the DAC to get involved, and at lunchtime too, was ominous. Turning to the MP, as they climbed in the back of the Ford, he suggested a lift back to Westminster. 'I'll jump out in Broadway and Shawcross can drop you back at the Commons.'

As Shawcross headed into Royal Hospital Road, towards Pimlico, Young asked him about the peer's book. 'You found nothing on St Oliver's desk like a manuscript?'

'Nothing like that, but it may be in one of the locked drawers. Do you want me to check with the Incident Room? They'll have cleared the contents of the study by now.'

'It'll wait. What did you make of him?' he asked North.

'Some of the stuff about the book sounds a bit ropy to me,' replied the MP. 'For someone who has never written before, to produce a decent-sized book in a year without editorial help is quite unusual.'

'So what kind of document are we looking for?' asked Young.

'If it's a properly finished manuscript, you're probably talking about two to three hundred pages, double-spaced.'

'So it's going to be bulky . . . A big, noticeable item. But in your judgement he's simply not up to writing a book on his own?'

'For someone like him, who's not a professional, his publisher would arrange a ghost-writer to help out. I can't see him completing a book on time without real assistance.'

'Particularly pondlife like him who may be distracted by a habit,' agreed Young, as he dug Shawcross in the shoulder. 'You were in the Drug Squad once. Did he look clean to you?'

'Not a chance, guv. Did you see the way he drew on

that cigarette? Nervous as hell. Couldn't bear the idea
of what he would probably call the fuzz or the filth
sitting in his drum, only a few feet away from his
stash. Looked to me as though a serious amount of
white stuff has been up his nose.'

'Let's get a warrant and when he comes in this
afternoon send a team in to turn it over. If we find
his stash we can apply some pressure. He obviously
knows more than he's saying. Wait till I get to the
Yard and inform the local nick by landline. It's Lucan
Place, isn't it?'

Shawcross grunted an affirmative. 'The little sod'll
be swimming in reporters by the time he's released
on bail. Don't suppose his landlady'll be too pleased
but it'll teach her a lesson,' said Young.

North remained silent. He was less than comfortable about the Chief Inspector's tactics and felt
slightly responsible. Fortunately, the subject changed.
'And what about Lady St Oliver? On the game, do
you reckon?'

'Surely not,' protested North. 'She may fancy herself
as a courtesan, perhaps, but not a hooker.'

Young shrugged his shoulders. 'Wasn't it the fashion
for all dukes to marry dancing girls in the not-too-
distant past?'

'Sigi was neither a duke nor an aristocrat,' sniffed
the MP in mock disapproval. 'I think she's too smart
to lie to the police about something like her marriage
lines, which can be verified so easily.'

'Not as easy as you think,' disagreed Young. 'Am I to
ask to see her marriage certificate? She could refuse. I

can almost hear the complaint to the Commissioner now. Police harassment of a widow. And how do we check on some ceremony held on some island in Italy? I think she could be bluffing. Still, St Oliver's solicitor will know. He'll tell us. That's something else you can do while I'm at the Yard.'

'Simons & Simons, in the City. I've got it,' acknowledged Shawcross as he raced up Birdcage Walk and turned sharply into Queen Anne's Gate.

'And see what we have on Lord Rendell. Wasn't he an MP?' he asked North.

'He was one of Ted Heath's ministers. He resigned when he was caught with a call-girl.'

'Nice friends, Aldworth has,' remarked Young, slyly. 'Lunching with Fergie, knowing Tory MPs by their Christian names. Where will it all end?'

North ignored the pointed remark and moments later they were in Broadway, opposite the main entrance to New Scotland Yard. Young slipped out the rear door and waved to North. 'I'll catch up with you later, at the Commons.'

Chapter Four

The Life Peer

Detective Chief Inspector Young made his way to the most northerly end of the ugly glass and concrete block that accommodated the Special Branch. He pushed through the revolving doors and past the cabinet displaying the book of remembrance, open at a page bearing the names of the most recent police officers to have lost their lives in the line of duty, showed his warrant card to the uniformed civilian security guard and then took the furthest bank of lifts to the sixth floor.

The DAC's secretary motioned him through her small room and into a larger, corner office overlooking the traffic lights at the corner of Victoria Street.

'Thank you for coming so quickly,' said the Deputy Assistant Commissioner, rising from behind his wide desk. 'These two gentlemen are from, er, the Security Service.' He had to catch himself from saying MI5. 'Mr de Gruyt is the case officer, and Mr Bicton is the legal adviser.'

The DCI shook hands with both men. De Gruyt looked as though he was around fifty, balding, perhaps nearing retirement. His colleague was much younger, in his late thirties, with red hair. When Peter Phelan resumed his seat his visitors sat in the chairs placed before his desk.

'I had wanted a briefing about St Oliver's background,' opened Young, 'but I hadn't expected action this fast.'

'I think Mr de Gruyt can help you there,' said the DAC, 'but we are also concerned about the Lithuanian journalist, Viktor Strelets. Perhaps you could let us know where your enquiries have taken you so far.'

'As you know, Lord St Oliver was murdered yesterday afternoon, in the House of Lords. His body was found by the Bishop of Donnington, whom we interviewed this morning.'

'Anything useful?' interrupted Phelan.

'Not exactly, sir. He's an elderly cleric but he seems to have had strong links with the Baltic community in this country.' Young glanced across at de Gruyt, but he was taking notes and betrayed no sign of ever having heard of the Bishop. 'He denies having known St Oliver but we may have to see him again.'

'Why so?' asked Phelan.

'Mainly because he admits to having known Viktor Strelets. Strelets was in the Lords at the exact time St Oliver was killed. I haven't interviewed him yet but I wanted to pull him in this afternoon. I can't overlook the possibility of a connection between the murdered man, the Bishop and Strelets.'

'When you say "pull him in",' interrupted Bicton, 'do you mean arrest him?'

'Not exactly,' replied Young. 'I was going to invite him to come in and assist me with my enquiries. Have you any objection?'

Phelan intervened. 'These gentlemen are here to help and advise us,' he said, sounding conciliatory. 'They just want to give us a few pointers. There's no question of, er, interfering with your investigation. You must conduct that as you think fit. You are the officer in charge.'

'Well,' said Young, somewhat mollified, 'it would help if I could know about St Oliver's background. All I know at present is that he comes from Lithuania, has served some time and has a nasty neck wound.'

The DAC nodded to the Security Service legal adviser. 'Perhaps Mr Bicton can help.'

Bicton opened a buff file. 'You may like to take some notes,' he said. 'This information is classified, so it should not be disclosed to anyone outside this room. It is for your knowledge only.'

'Sigismund Rosenbaum was probably born in Lithuania. We can't be sure but in his naturalization papers he stated the place as Ukmerge, which is between Kaunas and Vilnius. It's not far from the Polish border. He said his parents were dead, victims of Nazi atrocities, and gave his religion as Jewish. He was processed as a displaced person at a camp in the British Zone in November 1945 and he declared that he had not served in any German military or auxiliary units. He underwent the usual denazification procedure and was admitted to this country in February 1946 and employed by the government until September 1948, in Scotland and then in Devon. He applied for British citizenship in January 1947 and this was granted in June 1948, following the usual checks. He then changed his name by deed poll to Rose.

'He came to the notice of the Security Service in 1968 when he started to entertain a vice consul at the Soviet embassy who was suspected of being a professional intelligence officer. He was seen with a view to obtaining his assistance in regard to the Soviet, but he declined to help and broke off the contact.

'The other entries on his file are police notations which I'm sure you have. It's really just his criminal conviction for fraud.'

'Well, that seems very straightforward,' said Phelan. 'Perhaps we can now deal with Strelets.'

'Just a moment,' intervened Young. 'I have a couple of questions. Has St Oliver ever been suspected of complicity in war crimes, or has his name been included on any list produced by the Soviets?'

'Not as far as we are aware,' replied Bicton cautiously, 'but neither is really an issue for us. Our terms of reference are very strictly drawn, and the Foreign Office would probably be in a better position to give a more categoric answer. Do you mind telling me why you ask?'

'Because it has been suggested to me that the Soviets are in the habit of denouncing their political opponents as fugitives from Russian justice. Apparently Moscow have submitted lists of a rather dubious nature naming people they regard as war criminals who are living in Britain.'

'Yes, well, that's really not our province,' said Bicton dismissively,

'Very well,' accepted Young. 'Here's a question that you definitely can answer, then. Has St Oliver been either an anti-Communist activist or suspected of pro-Soviet sympathies?'

Bicton chose his words carefully, as was his custom. As one of the Service's main interfaces between what was a clandestine body and the rest of Whitehall, his job required an exacting degree of circumspection and tact. On some occasions his brief was damage limitation, picking up the pieces following some mishap. Today he had an equally delicate task. 'To our knowledge, St Oliver never played a part in *émigré* politics in this country, but after our approach to him over the vice consul an entry was made on his file to indicate the possibility of a Soviet link. It was never followed up, and we have nothing recorded against him in terms of political membership. In other words, he has never been a card-carrying member of the CPGB or any other organization that might bring him to our notice.'

'And this employment by the government in 1946 ... What was it?'

'He was a civilian language teacher for the Royal Air Force,' said Bicton.

'In Scotland and Devon?'

'Yes, at RAF Crail in Fife, and then RAF Bodmin.'

'And where was the DP camp in Germany? Not Bremen, by any chance?'

'No, it was at Oldenburg.'

'Is there a record of a British officer named Thresher interviewing Rosenbaum?'

'Not that I can see from the file, but I'll check and let you know. Who's this man Thresher?'

'He is the Bishop of Donnington, who says he never met St Oliver. However, he was based in Bremen after the war, and admits he handled refugees. I find the coincidence a little implausible.'

Bicton made no comment on the detective's observation. 'My colleague can tell you about Strelets,' he said, turning to de Gruyt.

The case officer needed no notes. 'Strelets is a professional intelligence officer, a member of the Third Department of the First Chief Directorate of the KGB, holding the rank of major. That's the KGB's foreign intelligence branch. He's an experienced agent-runner who has been operating in this country for six years. He's urbane, charming, and not above passing himself off as a critic of the Communist system. We recognize him for exactly what he is: a dangerous opponent who exploits his cover as the TASS agency correspondent to the maximum. As you would expect, he has been subject of a lengthy surveillance operation and we know he is having an affair with his secretary. Our hope is that he may compromise himself and thereby give us an opportunity to make our pitch.'

'What sort of a pitch is that?' enquired the detective.

'Most probably defection, but ideally we should like

to run him as a source for a while.'

'So are you saying that you don't want me to question him about the murder of St Oliver?' demanded Young, his hackles rising again.

'That is entirely a matter for you,' replied de Gruyt. 'My only request is that you keep me informed of everything that happens concerning him. As far as I'm concerned, you can arrest him on any charge you like. It's just that I would like to know a little ahead of the media.'

'So you won't interfere if I decide to interview Strelets this afternoon?'

'I say again, these decisions are entirely a matter for you. But I should welcome the opportunity to hear what Strelets has to say. He's a resourceful individual, well versed in counter-surveillance techniques, and no doubt a skilled adversary in the interrogation room. But I doubt he is your murderer. It's not his style.'

'Then what is?' asked Young.

'Political pressure, threats to the families of target expatriates still behind the Iron Curtain, perhaps a little coercion and blackmail, but no rough stuff. The modern KGB is too refined for that kind of business.'

'And why would Strelets be interested in St Oliver?'

'That I don't know. I can only say that his name has not come up in any of the, er, technical coverage we have utilized.'

Young liked the euphemism for tapping Strelets' telephone and bugging his home. 'One final question. If Strelets is such a danger to the state, why hasn't he been thrown out?'

'It's the devil-you-know principle. If Strelets is expelled he would be replaced, but it might take us a while to identify which Soviet journalist, banker, chauffeur, diplomat or member of the Trade Delegation was the new KGB officer. If Strelets oversteps the mark we'll run him out of the country, but provided he obeys the rules he can stay. And if he's tempted to stay permanently, we can arrange that too.'

'A pension and a house in Godalming,' remarked Young contemptuously.

'It's not much more than a supergrass would receive,' retorted de Gruyt. 'Information from defectors is quite the best way of corroborating intelligence from other sources. If Strelets can be persuaded to defect, he'd be quite a catch.'

'But not at the price of letting him off a murder charge,' said the Chief Inspector firmly. As he said it, he realized that Phelan was on his feet. The conference was at a close. De Gruyt handed him an office number and a mobile, and expressed his gratitude for the detective's co-operation. Bicton shook hands and insincerely expressed the hope of meeting again. Moments later, Young was in the lift heading for the lobby, conscious that the meeting had not gone well. He wondered whether, if the inquiry had not involved such a high-profile victim, a call might not have been made to the Assistant Commissioner Crime, resulting in his transfer to 'a less demanding role', or perhaps even an extended period of sick leave. But Young was confident that Phelan wouldn't pull that stunt and risk the adverse publicity.

It was only as Young emerged from the lift and saw Shawcross in the lobby that another thought occurred to him. Of course MI5 didn't want to *prevent* Strelets from being interviewed and charged ... that's actually what they probably wanted. What better lever to use against him? Threaten to frame him on a murder charge, and then offer him a way out.

'There's bad news and bad news and then some more,' opened Shawcross. 'Forensic have come up with nothing on St Oliver's body, and there's no Aldworth manuscript among St Oliver's possessions. We've been through the entire flat and Lady St Oliver denies ever having seen it. Furthermore, the doorman is positive that when Aldworth arrived yesterday morning, he wasn't carrying anything.'

'That's not bad news, that's good,' replied Young as they negotiated the revolving doors. 'Anything else?'

'The pathologist's preliminary report has arrived. St Oliver had mumps in his youth, and was sterile.'

'So Lady St Oliver is rather more religious than we gave her credit for,' answered Young.

'How so, guv?' asked Shawcross, mystified.

'Have you never heard of the immaculate conception?' asked Young as he climbed into the back of the Ford.

DCI Young collected North from the Members' Entrance of the Commons in New Palace Yard, and on the way through early westbound rush-hour traffic to Queen's Gate brought him up to date on what had transpired since they had parted outside Scotland Yard.

'The FBI have traced Sigi's first two wives. One died of an overdose at her home in Locust Valley, Long Island, nine years ago. One lives in Cuernavaca, in Mexico, but is supposed to be travelling in Europe. As for his third wife, Huddersfield CID have interviewed Maisie and she's signed a statement. She says she was running a stall at an NSPCC bring-and-buy fair all day, so she seems to be in the clear. She claims she's not particularly resentful of her husband, although he was apparently unfaithful on their honeymoon. The last straw was his affair with a nanny and his arrest in Malta. They had no children and they separated. Not much in the way of motive and on the face of it no opportunity unless there's collusion. There is no record of her being at the Lords yesterday.'

'But there wouldn't anyway,' remarked the MP. 'Visitors have to fill out forms for seats in the Strangers' Gallery, but there is no identity check. If she did slip down to London, perhaps on the train, she could easily have joined the queue for the Lords like the rest of the public.'

'Far-fetched,' objected Young. 'She couldn't have been certain of reaching the top of the queue on a popular day, and if Susie says there's been no contact between them, how did she know Sigi would be there? Then you've got the obstacle of her leaving the gallery at the exact moment that Sigi chose to walk into the Not Content Lobby. No, she's not in the frame. Susie, on the other hand, might be. Sigi wasn't the father of her baby and as for the wedding lines, her solicitor at Simons & Simons has got in on the act and has promised me a statement first thing tomorrow morning. He'll be burning the candlewax late tonight.'

'And I saw on the ticker-tape that you've busted Jonti Aldworth.'

'He's sweating it out at Rochester Row,' grinned the detective. 'It was all fair and square, with enough cocaine to put him away for a while. His shoes and clothes have been sent to forensic for examination.'

North made no comment. Quite obviously the police had not honoured Young's commitment to media silence, and once again Jonti's name would appear in banner headlines in the following morning's tabloids. He found Young's assurance that the raid had been 'fair and square' entirely unconvincing. Clearly the detective saw Aldworth, in much the same way as he saw the MP's own contribution, as a window into what would otherwise be a closed world. Jonti was a weak link, and evidently Young calculated that by the application of pressure on the peer he would disclose enough information to crack the case. The success of that strategy depended on the wretched viscount knowing something useful, and North did not share Young's confidence on that score. 'So you're convinced Aldworth is involved in the murder?' he asked.

'Not necessarily,' said the detective casually, who had been storing up his coup. 'It's just that he fabricated everything to do with his last meeting with St Oliver. That kind of thing makes me suspicious. When your viscount went to see his publisher, he was empty-handed. There was no manuscript. For all I know, there isn't one.'

What an idiot, thought the MP. It was typical of Jonti to make up a tale that could be disproved so easily. 'How did you get on with Special Branch?' he ventured, somewhat deflated.

'Not much on St Oliver,' lied Young with ease. 'He's never been accused of war crimes by the Soviets but he was processed in Germany at a refugee camp run by the British. The Yard is checking to see if we can link the Bishop to St Oliver. If so, the Bishop will have some explaining to do.'

'And that's it?' asked North with disbelief.

'Only some classified stuff about Strelets which you don't want to hear,' replied Young. 'Or you do, but I can't tell you. I think we should concentrate on Miss Susie. Obviously she's got a lover and if she's in Sigi's will she'll be in the frame again. What did you find out about Rendell?'

'I've arranged for you to have a drink with him in the Lords this evening, at six. He seemed quite shocked by the murder. They all do.' The car swung into Old Brompton Road and then took a further turn into Rosary Gardens where they were due for their re-scheduled meeting with Strelets. 'It's an improbable place for a nest of spies, but this is it,' announced Shawcross.

Strelets had been delayed by a television interview he had been recording in his own office at *Socialist Industry*, a Russian language weekly journal which enjoyed an enormous circulation within the Soviet Union but practically none outside. His visitors were asked to wait in the room occupied by the corres-

pondent. There was, apart from a rather ancient type-
writer and a small photocopier, nothing about it that
suggested any industry. The Buckingham Palace sou-
venir coffee mugs did not add credence to the idea
that Socialism reigned here either. It was untidily
furnished with a mixture of old bookshelves and
desks, and two modern chairs. After several minutes
of stilted conversation, subdued by the unspoken recognition that the premises were probably wired for
sound by the Russians if not the British, Strelets
strode into the room. He was smartly dressed, wearing what North guessed was an expensive Italian suit
and a very English polka-dot silk tie. His shirt looked
like Harvie & Hudson, and his shoes were unques-
tionably Church's.

'Welcome, gentlemen,' he boomed, with only the
slightest of accents, which might have been mistaken
for that acquired by a Frenchman who had spent too
long in Manhattan. 'Your very English murder has
turned me into something of a celebrity. That was
an NBC crew interrogating me about the Communist
perspective of the House of Lords. It will be coast to
coast tonight. Now I'm ready for your interrogation.'

Young made the introductions and explained that
North was assisting the inquiry as the personal representative of the Lord Chancellor. The journalist
was impressed.

'Was your presence in the Lords yesterday in any
way connected with Lord St Oliver?' opened the
detective.

'Only to the extent that the man calling himself

93

Rose was a war criminal, and I was sure he would be there for the debate,' declared Strelets. 'He had a big interest in stopping that law.'

'Can you explain your reference to Rose? Are you saying that wasn't his real name?'

'You didn't know?' asked Strelets innocently. 'I thought Special Branch knows everything?'

'I'm not a Special Branch detective,' bridled Young. 'Who do you say Rose really was? It is not a crime to change your name from Rosenbaum to Rose. Many people prefer to anglicize their surnames.'

'Rosenbaum was just a name. I think the real Rosenbaum was killed by the Nazis during the Great Patriotic War. I don't know. He was one of millions.'

'Very well,' said Young, rephrasing the question. 'Who do you say was the person who called himself Sigismund Rosenbaum?'

'He was Orobinsky, Yacov. There is no doubt. Your Special Branch knows this. He was the Jew Orobinsky.'

'So let me get this straight,' said Young slowly. 'The man who was murdered yesterday, whom we call Sigismund St Oliver, formerly Sigismund Rose by deed poll, and originally Rosenbaum, was born with the name Yacov Orobinsky.'

'Of course,' shrugged the journalist. 'You have known this for years.'

'Let's clarify that again,' said Young slowly, as though he was unsure that Strelets' comprehension of English was quite as thorough as his accent suggested. 'Why do you believe I know this to be the case?'

'Because you are Special Branch . . .' He held up his hand as if to prevent a denial, which was certainly imminent. 'I understand you have to pretend you are not Special Branch. But I know you are. I think your colleague here' – and he gestured to Shawcross – 'is MI5 man, but I don't mind. I play the game for you. Orobinsky was a war criminal. Special Branch protect him. I know, you know. Now you want to find his killer, and I am willing to help. Tell me what you want to know. I give full co-operation.'

Young looked exasperated, but clearly he wasn't in the mood to debate his non-membership of the Branch. He was also irritated by the smile which had passed briefly across Shawcross's face. Shawcross had shared North's amusement at the correspondent's certainty that he was in the presence of a Security Service officer. 'What evidence have you that Rosenbaum was a false identity?'

'But you have the evidence. You have sworn statements of witnesses. You have the confession of an SS soldier. You have the list of confirmed war criminals issued by the Simon Weisenthal Institute of Vienna. The question of identification is not in doubt.'

'Bear with me, Mr Strelets, but I have seen none of these things,' assured Young. 'What name was on this list of Simon Weisenthal's? Rosenbaum or Orobinsky?'

'Sure, it was Orobinsky. But Orobinsky is Rosenbaum. The man you call St Oliver. Anyway, who was Saint Oliver? I need to know for my feature article.'

'I have no idea,' murmured Young. 'According to what I have been told, Rosenbaum was born in some unpronounceable town halfway between Kaunas and

Vilnius. Are we talking about the same person?'

'Kaunas and Vilnius? No. Orobinsky was from Klai-
peda, the port that was once called Memel, far from
Kaunas. His father was a ship broker, his mother
a nurse.'

Young could see this avenue was not going to aid
identification. 'What is Orobinsky supposed to have
done?'

'Orobinsky was a war criminal.'

'What exactly does that mean?' pressed Young. 'Did
he fight against Stalin with Vlassov's army? What
did he do to be labelled a war criminal?'

'Vlassov's army?' laughed Strelets. 'This is ridiculous. Orobinsky was company commander in SS Police
Battalion. He killed hundreds, thousands of civilians
in occupied territory. He was mass murderer.'

'And Orobinsky was a Jew?' asked Young
incredulously.

'Sure, Orobinsky was Jew. That makes no difference. He killed women, Russian children.'

The detective was silent for a moment while he
absorbed this. 'What evidence have you that Yacov
Orobinsky changed his name to Rosenbaum?'

'We have legal document sworn by witness.'

'An eye-witness that could give first-hand evidence
and be cross-examined in a British court?' queried
Young sceptically. 'Nothing less would be acceptable.'

'Of course,' replied Strelets. 'When the papers were
made available to your authorities, his mother was
still alive.'

'Your witness was St Oliver's mother?' gasped

Young, unable to conceal his disbelief.

'Sure, his mother. Also his statement.'

'You had a statement from St Oliver?' repeated the detective, perplexed.

'Sure, his statement. Not sworn in front of prosecutor, but handwritten statement.'

'When did he sign the statement?'

'1967, I think. Maybe 1968.'

'And why did he sign it?'

'It was part of his mother's application for an exit visa. She wanted to emigrate. In the Soviet system exit visas are only granted to people who can demonstrate they will be supported in the West.'

'Do you have this document?' asked Young slowly.

'Not here. Your Foreign and Commonwealth Office has a copy.'

'And why didn't St Oliver's mother emigrate?'

'She died before the necessary papers had been completed. She was very old woman, but the identification was certain. Orobinsky was your Lord St Oliver.'

Young hesitated before starting a new tack. All his prepared questions had been thrown into disarray by Strelets' assertions, none of which he could believe to be true, because they were so contradicted by what he had been told in Phelan's office, and yet . . . 'When did you become aware that St Oliver's true name was Yacov Orobinsky?'

'I think I read it for the first time in the *Literary Gazette*, about six months ago.'

'Did you put the allegation to St Oliver himself?'

'No, I never met him.'

'To your knowledge, was he aware of the allegation?'

Strelets looked puzzled. 'He knew who he was. He has always known.'

'That's not what I mean. Did he see the article in the *Literary Gazette*? Did he know that his alleged change in identity was public knowledge?'

Strelets gave a shrug. 'I can't say. I don't know what newspapers he read.'

'Do you have a copy of the article?' asked Young. 'May I see it?'

'Sure. I have it somewhere. I will find it. I think in my office. You speak Russian?'

'No,' replied Young. 'And neither does my colleague, Detective Inspector Shawcross,' he added curtly.

'Fine,' smiled the TASS man. 'I get it when NBC TV leave.'

'Thank you,' replied the detective. 'What I don't quite understand is why you didn't confront St Oliver with the allegations against him. Why didn't you ask him if they were true?'

'Why ask?' said Strelets. 'The criminal Jew Orobinsky had the protection of the British government. He had been given citizenship by the government and he was a Lord. He is one of many war criminals protected by your government.'

'Can you tell me why you think the British government protects a war criminal?'

'Because the criminal Jew Orobinsky was a spy. A very useful spy.'

'You think Orobinsky, or St Oliver, spied for the British government?' Now Young was sure that

Strelets had stepped into the world of fantasy.

'Sure he was a spy. He was recruited by the British in Germany after the war. He was taken to England to be a spy.'

'According to the information I have,' replied the detective, 'Rosenbaum came to Britain as a refugee and taught languages for the Royal Air Force. That doesn't make him a spy.'

'Why does the Royal Air Force need to speak Russian?' countered Strelets. 'Orobinsky taught spies at special schools for spies. Sure, the school in Scotland was called Royal Air Force Crail, but that was disguise. The Government does not put up sign saying "School for Spies". But there are no aeroplanes at Crail. It is secret school.'

At the mention of RAF Crail, Young found himself believing Strelets again. It was a slightly different version of what Bicton had told him earlier in the afternoon, but it was not dissimilar. He wondered if he ought to have been more enquiring about the nature of St Oliver's work after the war for the government. And Strelets was right. Why would the RAF need Russian-speakers? Air-traffic control in occupied Germany? For pilots flying to Moscow? More likely it was for the examination of captured documents or perhaps the interrogation of prisoners. And that was the world of intelligence. 'What evidence have you that the work St Oliver did at Crail was to do with espionage?'

'Because Crail is famous in the Soviet Union. We know the spies who have been trained there. We know

who the instructors are. We have confessions of spies
infiltrated by the British into Latvia and Lithuania.
We have photographs. We know all about RAF Crail.
We know about Bodmin.'

'You say the same work was conducted at
Bodmin?'

'Sure, personnel at Crail move to Bodmin. The
training of spies is the same.'

'I see,' said Young thoughtfully, as he considered
the chronology of Orobinsky's metamorphosis from SS
monster into Rosenbaum the refugee. 'If we suppose
for a moment that you're right, and Orobinsky became
Rosenbaum in Germany after the war, why do you
think the British played any part in it? What was
to prevent Orobinsky from deceiving the authorities?
Others did.'

'Orobinsky became Rosenbaum while in the hands
of the British,' said Strelets. 'Of course British Intelligence knew he was Orobinsky. The British Special
Services wanted to fight the Soviet Union. It was
natural that they should rely on SS to train spies.
There was never any need to deceive the authorities.'

Despite what he was hearing, Young found it difficult to believe that war criminals could have been
consciously recruited by the intelligence services.
Whatever the expediency of employing Russian language teachers, he was sure they would have drawn
the line at former members of the SS. At least, he
thought he was sure. But if even a fraction of what
Strelets said was true, Bicton had been guilty of more
than just being disingenuous. He must have known

the truth. Or did he? Had he been duped too by an incomplete brief? When he cast his mind back to their conversation, there had been no mention of intelligence. He had not volunteered the names Crail and Bodmin until challenged about what Sigi had done for the government after the war. He felt like kicking himself for not asking more about exactly who in the RAF Sigi had been teaching.

'Perhaps we can go back to the time you say Orobinsky's mother applied to emigrate,' resumed Young. 'What can you tell me about that episode?'

'After the war Orobinsky resumed contact with his mother. His father had died in the war. She was alone and she applied for an exit visa. Yacov Orobinsky signed the legal papers to allow her to emigrate.'

'Where did Orobinsky sign these legal papers? In London?'

'Of course. If he was to return to Lithuania he would be arrested as war criminal.'

'And when these papers were signed in London, did this happen at the embassy? Did Orobinsky approach the embassy, or did the embassy find Orobinsky?'

'I do not know the details,' said Strelets dismissively, as if the point was insignificant, but Young could see several different scenarios emerging, all centred on an old widow living in poverty behind the Iron Curtain.

'And when did Orobinsky's mother die?' queried the detective.

'I don't have the date,' he replied. 'She was not in good health after the war.'

'I see,' said Young. 'But you never mentioned any of this to St Oliver himself?'

'Never. I am a journalist. If I approach St Oliver for an interview he would complain to Special Branch. Immediately, I am expelled for harassing a Lord. I am not so foolish.'

'But you have spoken to the Bishop of Donnington?'

'Ah, the Bishop. Yes, he is very interested in the affairs of the Baltic community. I have written about him once or twice.'

'Did you know he was in the Lords yesterday?'

'No, I did not. But he has retired. He is not a member of the House of Lords.'

'I know,' said Young with a trace of weariness. 'He has retired, but he does still go occasionally to the Lords. And he was there yesterday. You are quite sure you didn't see him, or speak to him?'

'Definitely,' said Strelets firmly.

'Can you tell me where you were yesterday...? All day?'

'I was in my office in the morning. Because of the time difference with Moscow I have to file my reports before midday. Then I had lunch at the Foreign Press Association in Carlton House Terrace to hear about the plans for the Channel Tunnel. Then I walked across St James's Park to the House of Lords for the war crimes debate.'

'What time did you arrive?'

'I went up to the Press Room at about three. I stayed until after the murder.'

'Did you leave the Press Room or the Press Gallery at any time?'

'Only to leave the building after the murder.'

'Did you speak to anyone on the way in or on the way out of the Lords?'

'I said hello to Ivan Lawrence in the Central Lobby. He has been very active in this Bill and he was going into the Lords too. There was nobody else until the policeman who took my name and address when I wanted to leave.'

'And where did you go when you left the Lords?'

'I came straight back here to write my story. This has been a big sensation.'

'I know,' murmured Young. 'Perhaps you could let me have this magazine article, and then I'll be in touch again if anything more arises.'

'I will see if my colleague from *Novosti* has finished his interview. Please wait a moment here.' He grinned engagingly as he slipped out of the door. 'You see, I have no secrets from Special Branch.'

'It's so typical,' observed Young with a sigh to North. 'He's convinced we're from the Branch.'

'You knew Sigi had been in the RAF?' whispered North accusingly.

'He wasn't in the RAF,' said Young firmly. 'We'll talk about this later. All I knew was that he'd been a languages teacher after the war. So what? All this spying malarky sounds a bit odd to me.'

A minute or two later Strelets returned, carrying two pieces of paper. 'Here is the article. It was published in December last year. I will make you a copy,' he said and placed the first sheet onto the Xerox machine in the corner.

'Perhaps you could make me a copy too,' asked North.

'Sure, no problem,' said Strelets, running off a second sheet for the MP. The print quality was not particularly clear, but the cyrillic characters were legible. 'Do you speak Russian?' he asked North.

'Hardly a word. My vocabulary is limited to *glasnost, perestroika* and *dozvadanyia*.'

'Well, your accent is good,' said the journalist untruthfully, amused to hear his own language. 'Have you been to Moscow?'

'Not yet, but I'd like to go.'

'We have another appointment,' interjected Young, as he took his copy of the *Literary Gazette* article. 'Thank you for your time, and I'm sure we'll be in touch again.' He turned to leave, with Shawcross already holding the door open.

'Any time,' answered Strelets cheerily. 'I must keep very good relations with Special Branch.'

As they sank into the back seat of the Ford, Young exploded with pent-up frustration. 'God, I find that man irritating. All this fucking Special Branch crap. He's not interested that a man's been murdered. His own countryman, too.'

'Strelets is Lithuanian as well?' asked North. 'Was that another part of your briefing?'

Young had been caught off-guard. North was nobody's fool, he thought. 'They warned me that Strelets might be an intelligence officer. Didn't you say you thought he was probably KGB?'

'And what about St Oliver and the RAF?' asked

North, ignoring the question. He was intrigued by the Branch's briefing, which he suspected had been rather more substantial than Young had told him.

'I was told about that too. Apparently St Oliver was used as a linguist after the war, but not for long. Strelets is just demonstrating his paranoia by all this talk of espionage. I can't really accept any of that.'

'But did the Branch say that St Oliver had been suspected of being a war criminal?'

'Definitely not,' recalled the detective with a trace of irritation. 'I asked the question about the list of suspects that the Bishop mentioned, but there was a flat denial.' As he remembered the scene in the DAC's office, he wondered whether he had really asked the right question. St Oliver's name had not appeared on a Soviet list, or so Bicton had said. But what about the name Orobinsky? Young had not known the name to mention it, and perhaps this had given the Security Service men an opportunity to be disingenuous. What would their answer have been if he had rephrased the question ... 'Was St Oliver's name, or any other alias used by him, on a Soviet list?' This was an issue he was determined to confront Bicton with, but he was not inclined to share his thoughts with the MP. He strongly suspected he had been duped, and he didn't like the idea. Nor did he want to advertise the fact.

'Back to the Commons,' instructed Young, as the MP flinched. 'We'll see Lord Rendell and then give Aldworth a lesson in social responsibility. Now, about Rendell. He was in the Commons, wasn't he?'

North accepted that the detective knew the answer already but wanted his memory refreshed about the scandal surrounding his resignation. 'He renounced his title when he was elected and sat in the Commons as Tony Haye. After his resignation he was given a life peerage so he returned to the Lords.'

'Is that usual?' asked Young.

'Peers have been able to disclaim their title since Tony Benn, who was then Viscount Stansgate, had the law changed in 1962. Several have followed his example, but it's usually only those who achieve Cabinet rank like Home and Hailsham who are granted life peerages and sent back upstairs.'

'So Rendell sits in the Lords as a life peer, and not as a hereditary peer.'

'Exactly,' agreed the MP. 'The overwhelming majority of members of the Upper House are hereditary peers, who are known as peers by succession. Less than half, only about 350 peers, are life peers. There's no difference in voting rights, but when Rendell dies the original title will pass to his nearest male heir.'

'And Rendell inherited his title from his father?'

North nodded. 'His father was killed in the war. I think he was a fighter pilot. Anyway, Tony became Lord Rendell while he was still at school.'

The Detective Chief Inspector's introduction to Lord Rendell was made by North in the Pugin Room, where the peer was sitting with a large gin and tonic. He had entered the small bar overlooking the Thames,

and had selected a seat in the window alcove, exactly
on time, but North and Young had been late, delayed
by evening traffic around Sloane Square and then
Victoria Station. North immediately recognized him
and guided Young around the leather armchairs to the
alcove. Although they had not been in the Commons
together, the MP knew Rendell by sight. He was, after
all, quite a public figure, if a reluctant one. He was
tall, immaculately dressed in a Jarvis & Hamilton
pinstripe suit, with knotted silk links in the double
cuffs of his pale blue Turnbull & Asser shirt. His hair
was speckled with grey over the temples, receding
only slightly as he approached sixty, and was swept
back with the help of some oil from Trumpers, with
one strand falling to his left eyebrow. As his two visitors approached, Rendell rose to his feet in welcome,
a quizzical smile developing on his face, lined and
windbeaten from a dozen Fastnet and Round the
Island races. An active commodore of the Royal Ocean
Racing Club, he had kept himself very fit, and he was
still a keen sportsman, shooting partridges in Spain
every year and salmon fishing in Alaska with John
King.

The detective made no apology for having made the
ex-minister wait. 'I understand you were once Lord
St Oliver's business partner,' opened Young, as he sat
down. 'What can you tell me about the man?'

'Sigi was never a partner,' corrected Rendell. 'He
published two of my books and I am under contract
for a third, but I was not a director of his company.'

'I understand that St Oliver cheated you.'

Rendell laughed. 'So you heard about that, did you? No, Sigi didn't cheat me, but he tried to. Let's just say we had a disagreement. Nothing serious, you know.'

When it came to money, thought North, nothing was ever serious with Tony Rendell. He possessed a brilliant brain but he was too much of a dilettante. He had easily mastered his briefs at the Despatch Box but had been bored by his ministerial posts in the Commons. He had a low threshold of boredom and therefore had been regarded by some of his colleagues as aloof and even arrogant. Despite this, he had proved himself a highly competent and articulate member of the Government, except when it had come to his own private life. Then, when his liaisons had been revealed, he had promptly resigned his seat and been curiously tongue-tied in a memorable interview with Robin Day. After that experience, Rendell had dropped from public view and concentrated on Clare, his mistress of longstanding, and his writing, at his Palladian villa outside Siena, returning to his Scottish estate during the shooting season and to London to attend the occasional debate in the Lords. The days of riotous parties at his St John's Wood home were long gone, as was the pretence that his marriage was intact.

'What exactly was the disagreement about?' pressed the detective.

'It was my biography of Morton. The *Sunday Times* bought the serial rights but Sigi tried to set the fee against the advance I'd been paid. He thought I wouldn't notice. Our lawyers exchanged letters, and that was the end of the matter.'

'So St Oliver paid you the money he owed,' concluded Young.

'He never did. His company went into receivership and I was left as one of the unsecured creditors.'

'But you said you're still writing a book for him,' protested the detective.

'I have no choice,' shrugged the peer. 'Sigi simply started another firm and bought the outstanding assets of the bust company from the liquidator. He never released me from the contract so I was stuck with him as my publisher. It's not the end of the world.'

'But he was responsible for your, er, fall from grace,' said Young, attempting and failing to choose the right words to describe Rendell's involvement with the scandal that brought about his resignation from the Government. Young's stab at tact made North cringe.

'That was a separate issue,' said Rendell, apparently unconcerned by the detective's gaucheness. 'I don't blame him for what happened. It was entirely my responsibility. As for the money, Sigi was predictable and I would have been disappointed if he had not tried to bilk me out of my royalties. The man was a rogue, not a crook.'

'There's a difference?' enquired the detective.

'Everyone knew what Sigi was like. He threw wonderful parties, knew everyone, was always fixing deals behind the scenes, making introductions, but he was a rascal, not a real villain. It wasn't as if you had to count your fingers after you'd shaken hands with him. Know what I mean?'

Young was intrigued at how the upper classes could mix so easily with those they benevolently termed 'scoundrels' who had served prison sentences. 'So even though St Oliver had been convicted at the Old Bailey, that made no difference to your relationship?'

'Not really. I don't go to his parties any more, but his crime was fraud. Nobody was robbed by Sigi, except his own shareholders, and he and the banks owned the majority.'

'And when his company went belly-up? Didn't you lose?'

'Of course. But the chief loser was Sigi himself, and perhaps the taxman. And Charles Hardington, of course. He had guaranteed Sigi's bank loan, and when he defaulted Hardington had to stump up, or so the story goes ... But he can afford it.'

'Is that Lord Hardington?'

'The very same. Ironical, of course,' he added as an afterthought. 'If Sigi hadn't obtained a discharge from his bankruptcy, he would still be alive now.'

'How so?'

'Bankrupts can't sit in the Lords. That's about the only disqualification. If Sigi hadn't paid his debts, he wouldn't have been in the Lords yesterday.'

'So were you really quite fond of, er, the "rogue",' said the detective with manifest disapproval.

'Sigi was a great character. He was huge fun to be with, always ready with a funny story told against himself. He had no pretensions, and never concealed his spell in prison. I remember once he told me about how he had been invited to Senegal to address a conference. Even though the subject was breast-feeding, and his French was almost non-existent, Sigi had gone along for the generous fee, the first-class travel and a few days in the sun. He thought the audience had been captivated and at the end of his speech he had asked the organizer how he had done. "Very interesting, but what a shame you didn't mention press freedom!" That was typical of Sigi. Never a dull moment.'

'So can you think of anyone who would have wanted to kill him?' asked Young, unconvinced.

'No more than a dozen,' joked the peer, although the detective was clearly unamused. 'I think the world is the poorer without Sigi, but I'm probably in the minority holding that opinion. Old Lord Staveley had no love for him, and there was always talk of him and Lady Gresham. He was an old goat and loved living dangerously. And what about the duchess? She never forgave him and I don't suppose he did either. I'm afraid your list of suspects in the Lords will be quite a long one, but it won't include me.'

Young turned to another subject. 'How well did you know St Oliver's wife?'

'Which one?' countered Rendell, with something approaching a leer. 'I only met Maisie once, I think. Susie I knew quite well, and I saw Madeleine only last week. Susie's quite a poppet.'

'So St Oliver really did marry her?' asked Young.

'That's a bit of a leading question, isn't it?' said the

peer archly. 'She told me he had made an honest woman of her, and I guessed that's what she meant.'

'And what about Madeleine?' added Young.

'She gave a dinner party at Mosimann's last week, on Tuesday, I think. She was on her way to Antibes. She's still very good looking, you know. Really delicious.'

'And she now lives in Mexico?' said Young.

'She spends most of her time there, but when she comes to London she stays at the Berkeley.'

'Do you know if she saw St Oliver when she was here?'

'I doubt it. She always kept away from him. She often said that whenever she bumped into him she checked her purse.'

'Do you know where she's staying in Antibes?' probed the detective.

'Some friends have taken a house there. She didn't mention who, but you can be sure it'll have a tennis court. She still plays every day.'

'And when is she due back in London?'

'I've really no idea, but you don't have to worry about her. She had a bad experience with Sigi, years ago, but there's no bitterness. She wouldn't have wished him any real harm. A serious case of herpes, yes, but absolutely nothing worse. You can rule her out.'

'And what about you?' invited the detective. 'Should I rule you out too?'

'No motive,' said Rendell expansively. 'We had our ups and downs, but I was rather fond of Sigi.'

'But you were in the Lords yesterday afternoon,' stated Young.

'I was,' agreed Rendell, 'but I don't remember seeing Sigi. I think your best bet is Liz Gresham. She's easily fierce enough to have sliced poor Sigi into little pieces.'

Chapter Five

The Ninth Earl

It was nearly half past seven when Young and North walked into the interview room. Between the end of their meeting with Lord Rendell and their arrival at Rochester Row the Incident Room had been instructed to trace Madeleine Franks in the South of France, and to arrange for an interview with Lord Hardington. 'Get on to Companies House and see what directorships St Oliver held, and ask the Official Receiver for his file on the Truscott & Sweeting crash,' ordered Young. 'I'll also want to see his bank records. See if his manager will co-operate, or whether he'll need a court order.'

On the way to Rochester Row Young speculated about the possibility of Rendell's guilt. 'He's the first real Lord we've interviewed,' he ruminated. 'If he's the murderer, does he get tried by his peers?'

North laughed. 'You mean exercise his right to a full trial in the Lords, and to be hanged with a silken cord?'

'I saw it in *Kind Hearts and Coronets*,' said the detective defensively. 'Every Lord had to shout his verdict. No nonsense with jury foremen or unanimous decisions.'

'Their Lordships only wear their ermine robes for state occasions like Coronation Day and the annual Opening of Parliament. All that business of trying treason and felony in the Lords went out years ago.' The MP smiled, and noticed that his companion looked disappointed by the news.

They arrived at the police station off Vincent Square and a youthful detective constable showed them to the interview room holding the prisoner. As soon as they entered, Jonti Aldworth looked up. He had been slouched across the only table in the room, his head resting on his folded arms. A picture of despair, he looked pleadingly at the MP.

'For Christ's sake, can't you get me out of here?' begged the wretched man. 'This is so obviously a frame-up. I had nothing to do with Sigi's murder.'

North remained silent, as he had been requested by the detective. 'Mr North is here only as an observer. He can't help you. The only person who can get you out of here is you, sir,' said Young as he strode across to the twin-deck tape-recorder and switched it on. 'Interview with Jonathan Aldworth, commencing nineteen twenty-seven,' he intoned, in compliance with the terms of the hated Police and Criminal Evidence Act. 'Detective Chief Inspector Young, Detective Inspector Shawcross, and Philip North MP present in the room. Now' – he turned to the prisoner – 'please

116

will you confirm that you have received a caution and you have declined the offer of a solicitor.'

'I don't need a bloody lawyer because I haven't done anything,' protested Aldworth.

'If that is an affirmative, please say so,' said Young firmly.

'I confirm I've been cautioned and I don't want a poxy solicitor,' stated the Viscount.

'You are aware that substances taken from your flat under warrant are now being analysed,' said Young. 'If they prove to be controlled drugs, you will face a long custodial sentence.'

'There were no drugs at the flat,' insisted Aldworth. 'Phil, you've got to believe me.' North remained silent.

'You may also be facing a charge of obstruction or perhaps conspiracy to pervert the course of justice.'

Aldworth looked up sharply. 'What the hell are you talking about?'

'We've checked your tale about seeing St Oliver yesterday morning, and we have confirmed that you arrived empty-handed, and you gave him no manuscript. Your statement to me this afternoon was a complete fabrication.'

Aldworth looked crestfallen. 'I do have a book contract,' he conceded, 'but I had decided against writing it.'

'Then why did you lie?'

'I thought that if I told you we had argued you might think I had killed the old bastard. But I didn't.'

'So what really happened?'

'I told Sigi I wouldn't do the book. It was already

overdue and he'd been pestering me for the first few chapters. When he called me to his flat I simply told him that I'd changed my mind. I knew after I'd signed the contract that I'd regret it. He wanted as much dirt as possible. It didn't matter who got hurt. I just couldn't do it.'

'And what was St Oliver's reaction?'

'Can't you guess? He went ballistic. He was furious.'

'Was that all?' pressed the detective.

'He gave me a choice. Either I produced a manuscript or he wanted the money back.'

'How much?'

'When we signed the contract he gave me ten thousand pounds. Then he advanced me another six. He wanted sixteen thousand pounds, plus the interest.'

'Which you don't have,' said Young.

'Not a chance. I told him so, but he threatened to sue me. If he did I'd be bankrupted and my father would disinherit me.'

'And how did you leave matters?'

'I had no choice. There was no way I could write the book. I hadn't even started it. Nor could I pay him back. So I decided to call his bluff and see if he would take me to court. What else could I do?'

'Kill him, perhaps?' suggested the detective.

'I didn't kill him,' moaned the peer. 'I admit we parted company yesterday morning on bad terms, but the thought of bumping him off never crossed my mind. I had to gamble that Sigi would be unwilling to bring proceedings against me. He knows I don't have the money and he knows enough about my family to realize that my father would never bail me out. He hasn't in the past and he wouldn't lift a finger to sort out my problems with Sigi. But I reckoned Sigi would think twice before he started brawling with me in public.'

'And why is that?' asked Young casually.

'Because I've got too much on him. I know what a slimeball he really is.'

'And what exactly is this knowledge you have? I think the time has come for you to share it with me.'

Aldworth looked uncertain. 'If I tell you everything about Sigi, will you guarantee my release, and no charges?'

'Certainly not,' replied the DCI. 'I can't make deals. However, if I think you have been completely candid with us, I will make sure my views reach the right quarters. Any charges you face concerning drugs found in your flat are not for me to decide. Tell me what you know, and I'll do what I can to help.'

North winced at the detective's patent insincerity, and wondered how Jonti could even consider agreeing to such terms. But he could see that the peer's son was desperate. Was he being tortured by his habit? North averted his eyes from the spectacle of the younger man's torment and watched as the policemen prepared for Jonti's statement. But he had under-estimated him.

Aldworth's eyes narrowed. 'If I tell you about crimes that I might have been involved in, will you agree not to prosecute?'

Now it was Young's turn to hesitate. 'Are you saying

that in relation to St Oliver you might have been involved in a crime?'

'Well, let's speak hypothetically. Supposing I have a friend who became involved in something illegal, with a person the police are interested in, could the friend reveal what he knows without the risk of incriminating himself?'

'If you are trying to tell me that you sold drugs to St Oliver,' sighed the detective, 'it won't come as a great surprise to me. And I doubt we would even refer the matter to the Crown Prosecution Service.'

'No, not drugs. Supposing the friend was, er, part of a cover-up, over a death.' Young leaned forward and was about to interrupt. 'Not St Oliver's death,' explained Aldworth hastily. 'Someone else, and St Oliver was involved. Could the friend have immunity?'

The DCI deliberated for a moment. 'Let me put it this way,' he said. 'If you don't tell me everything, and I mean *everything*, I will make it my business to ensure you serve a very long stretch. And I'm talking about Durham, not Ford Open. This will be serious, hard time. Have you got the message? Now spit it out. Whose death were you and St Oliver involved in?'

Aldworth was deflated. A moment earlier there had been a gleam of hope in his eyes. He had been trying to make a deal, but Young had toughed it out, and North could see that Jonti was broken. Young saw it too, and softened his approach. 'Start at the beginning. How did you meet St Oliver?'

'It was when I was up at Oxford. St Oliver had been invited by the Union to debate a motion on

prison reform. It was a great evening and I was roped
in with a few others after the debate to take him to
dinner. He always started with the same joke, about
how he often opened Lord Olivier's letters by mistake,
and accepted his speaking engagements. His speech
was tremendous and the dinner was terrific too. We
went to the Saraceno, and there were about eight of
us. Usually the Union foots the bill, but he paid for
everyone. All I knew about him was what I had read
in the papers, but he was completely different. He
told us that he had a house near Stanton Harcourt,
and invited us to a party the following weekend. He
told us to bring who we liked, within reason, but he
didn't mind extra girls if they were good looking.'

'I think we all went, but we didn't take any extra
girls. We just thought he was an old lech, but his
party was great. Unlimited booze, masses of food and
he had one room set up as a cinema, showing cartoons
all night. Everyone was smashed, and we had a really
good time. He had these wild parties practically every
weekend in the summer term.'

'And you supplied the drugs?' asked Young.

'Not exactly. Everyone there was doing coke and
stuff. You'd be surprised who else was there. I took
some organic mescalin one time, and shared it
around, but most of the guests who were into that
had scored their own before they arrived. It really
was a wild scene. The house had about twelve bed-
rooms, and they were all in use.'

'By whom?' probed Young.

'Sigi's guests. He provided girls for those who'd

arrived alone for the weekend.'

'Do you know who they were?'

'Mainly Sigi's business contacts. The only two I recognize now are Tony Rendell and Charles Hardington.'

'Is that Lord Hardington?' enquired Young, as though he had not heard the name before.

Aldworth nodded with enthusiasm. 'He was one of Sigi's regulars, but you wouldn't think so to see him nowadays. He lost a lot when the company crashed, but he certainly enjoyed himself with Sigi's girls.'

'And in the midst of all this festivity someone died?'

'Yeah. Leander Byng OD'd. I found her.'

'And this was at St Oliver's house at Stanton Harcourt?'

'Oh no. She only went to one party. This happened a while later.'

'And how was St Oliver involved in her death?'

'The Coroner's verdict was misadventure, because of the overdose, but in fact Leander committed suicide.'

'How do you know?' asked Young gravely.

'This is the heavy part,' gulped Aldworth. 'Leander told me that Sigi had raped her. It had happened at his house during the party she went to. I didn't really believe her, and told her to forget it.'

'But she didn't?' added the detective.

'She left a suicide note blaming St Oliver. She thought she might be pregnant and she was petrified.'

'And what happened?'

'I found her, and I found her letter.'

'But you never told the police about the letter?'

'The police thought she had accidentally overdosed after a party. In fact we had been to a party, up in Summertown, but she seemed depressed and left quite early. She had a room in my girlfriend's house in the Iffley Road, and I walked in on her in the morning. We had arrived home in the early hours, and we didn't check on her. I suppose we should've, but we didn't. She died all alone. Anyway, the police always handled the case as an overdose, not a suicide.'

'And you gave evidence at the inquest?'

'Yeah. I said she'd been at the party, which was true, and I agreed that there had been drugs there. I said I couldn't remember much else.'

'But why didn't you give Leander's letter to the police?'

'Because my first instinct had been to give it to Sigi. I owed him a lot, and in those days I thought of him as a really good friend. This was my way to pay him back for all the good times. Once I'd handed the letter over to Sigi, I couldn't really tell the police about it. He might have made any kind of wild accusations, and I might have been blamed for giving Leander the drugs.'

'Added to which,' said the detective, 'you had no proof. Or did you?'

Aldworth nodded. 'Before I gave the letter to Sigi I had a sort of sixth sense. I took a photocopy. I never told him, but I thought it might be, you know, like an insurance policy.'

'And you still have it?' demanded Young earnestly.

'Yeah. I suppose as a last resort I would have sent

a copy of it to Sigi to shut him up.'

'And what were the accusations you thought St Oliver might have made against you?'

'I suppose blackmail. But it wouldn't have been true. I swear I never told Sigi I'd kept a copy. I never told anyone.'

'And where is it now?'

'It's at my bank . . . Coutts in Cadogan Place.'

'And in spite of Leander's death, you stayed friendly with St Oliver?'

'Not really. He knew I was short of money and after my car crash I had a habit to feed. He gave me the book contract, so I suppose I had to keep in touch with him. I never went to any of his parties, though.'

'Do you know what St Oliver did with Leander's original note?'

'No, but I guess he destroyed it.'

'And you're certain you've never told anyone else about Leander's suicide?'

'Certain. I knew that the whole thing was dynamite.'

'And have you anything else to add?'

Aldworth shrugged. 'That's it. Now, when can I leave?'

'Not for a while yet,' said Young as he turned towards the door. 'I think we'd better have a word about this,' he said to Shawcross and North. A few minutes later they were in the Incident Room, on the first floor of the police station.

'I get the impression this isn't bullshit,' announced Young. 'What do you feel?'

Shawcross nodded, and North made an observation. 'This might explain why St Oliver commissioned Aldworth to write a book. He could keep tabs on his aspiring author and remove anything indiscreet from the text. Furthermore, he could exercise complete control over anything Aldworth said to the press while the book was being prepared, and perhaps even afterwards.'

'So by giving Aldworth a publishing contract, he was effectively controlling everything he said about Leander's death,' noted Young.

'St Oliver could have prevented Jonti from ever saying anything about the affair, and used breach of copyright as an argument with the newspapers, instead of libel. It would have been far more effective.'

'So we need to see a copy of the contract,' agreed Young. 'We should also get the file on Leander Byng's death from the Thames Valley force.'

'You're not going to re-open the inquest?' asked North, visibly horrified.

'Not necessarily. But I want to check the facts. I still don't trust our Viscount.'

'Because it lets him off the hook?' queried the MP. 'If this is all true, he had no motive to kill St Oliver. If anything, he held a trump card against St Oliver. There's no way he would have risked taking Jonti to court, knowing that Jonti had the goods on him.'

'But did he know?' asked Young. 'Aldworth says he never told St Oliver he'd kept a Xerox of the suicide note.'

'But somebody as shrewd as St Oliver wouldn't have

wanted to take the risk. I think he'd have assumed Jonti had taken that basic step of self-preservation.'

'So we are really no nearer solving the murder,' observed Young. 'Aldworth's statement merely serves to make him a less likely suspect. It doesn't put anyone else in the frame.'

'What about Lord Hardington?'

Young looked sceptical. 'Not much of a motive, and he's not on the list of peers who attended the Lords yesterday, but we'd better see him first thing in the morning. Shawcross, can you make the arrangements, and I'll take Mr North back to the Commons. Then we'll get Aldworth to sign a formal statement.'

Lord Hardington received his three visitors in his office over his gallery in Bond Street. It was half past nine and the police had made an appointment with Simons & Simons in the City at ten-thirty. Young was anxious to see Susie St Oliver's solicitors and was frustrated at having been made to wait for fifteen minutes in the gallery, staring at what he regarded as a hideous Francis Bacon. When North had told him of its value he had been uncomprehending. 'I'd pay good money to keep that out of my house!' he had exclaimed. 'Anybody with that under the same roof would have sleepless nights.'

'You see what I mean,' said Shawcross in a stage whisper. 'It's the Lucan factor. Earls make him feel uneasy.'

Young scowled. 'I did some homework last night. Did you know that peers can't be arrested on civil charges forty days before the Lords sit, and forty days afterwards? It's ridiculous.'

'Not any more,' corrected North. 'There's only one advantage to being a peer these days ... They're exempt from jury service. On the negative side, you're classed with lunatics and felons and disbarred from voting. So it's not all pomp and privilege.'

Young snorted his disapproval. 'Jury service is a civic duty,' he commented.

'Oh, I forgot,' countered North. 'Felons, lunatics, peers ... and police officers. All the rest of us can sit in judgement on our fellow citizens.'

When they were eventually ushered into Hardington's office, by a very attractive, long-legged young woman dressed in a short Chanel suit who described herself as 'Charles's assistant', the Ninth Earl had been charm personified.

'I'm Charles Hardington. I'm so sorry to have kept you waiting. I have an important Japanese investor who had changed his mind about the auction in Monte Carlo next week. He was just leaving his office for the evening and you can't talk business to the Japanese at home. Please forgive me. I gather you want to have a word about poor old Sigi St Oliver.'

He was smooth, beautifully dressed, in a light Savile Row charcoal grey suit. His shirt was dark blue, but with a white collar, and when his left cuff rode up it revealed the small square face and Roman numerals of an original Cartier Tank watch on a crocodile strap, one of those made for tank commanders during the Great War. His accent had a

slight transatlantic twang. North recalled that before
Hardington had inherited the title from a distant
cousin, the Eighth Earl, and founded Blenheim Fine
Art, he had worked for Sotheby's in Park Avenue,
specializing in modern art. His talent at picking living
artists was phenomenal, as was his personal collection. Although he had been bequeathed 52,000 acres
of Gloucestershire, the estate had not had much cash.
Accordingly he was known to live rather unosten-
tatiously, sharing his small London town house in
Eaton Terrace with his long-time girlfriend, his mildly
alcoholic wife preferring country life in Gloucestershire where she organized an annual showjumping
event. It was a marital arrangement that caused neither any embarrassment, even when the Earl was
photographed with his mistress by the ever-discreet
Barry Swabe for the *Tatler* or *Harpers*. Still known to
his friends as 'CD', his initials before his cousin's
death, his circle of friends was more international
than English, with the Rothschilds, the Agnellis and
the Kennedys among those with whom he preferred
to spend his holidays.

In his late fifties, Hardington personified the new,
post-war aristocracy that had been brought up on a
combination of traditional British ordinariness and
a jet-set lifestyle: part of August was spent on a con-
ventional family holiday in Bembridge, with the
remainder devoted to Southampton, Long Island, but
in the winter his preference was for the Corviglia
Club in St Moritz with the Heinekens, Thyssens and
Stavros Niarchos, and then a week at Mick Jagger's

bamboo house on the beach in Mustique, rather than the *arrivistes* of the Eagle Club of Gstaad and St James's, Barbados. Always tanned, and invariably accompanied by a girl half his age, CD was unfailingly courteous. Whereas Tony Rendell was widely regarded as a shit by his contemporaries, especially where women were concerned, few were ever critical of the art dealer who had fathered three children and was thought to have had at least another pair illegitimately. As for the Lords, Hardington rarely attended and had not made his maiden speech. He had been heard to tell the anecdote about the peer who had a nightmare that he was speaking in the Upper House and woke to find it was true. 'There are more than a hundred and fifty earls in the Lords,' he usually said when challenged on the subject of his silence, 'so there's more than enough hot air already without me adding to it.' Yet his attitude was curiously contradictory, for he had taken a lot of trouble to persuade the Committee for Privileges of the authenticity of his claim to inherit his cousin's earldom and had undergone an unusually lengthy process of verification before finally taking the oath of allegiance.

DCI Young made the introductions. 'I understand that you were once Lord St Oliver's partner, and you knew him as well as anyone,' he opened. 'Perhaps you can tell me about your relationship.'

'I was Sigi's partner and a director of Trustcott & Sweeting. Although I provided some of the working capital, I was mostly a non-executive director. He was responsible for the day-to-day management and the catalogue's general and fiction list, and I supervised the art list. I guess we did about two or three art books a year. It was small stuff, but high quality. Colour printing in those days was not as easy as it is now.'

'How did you meet?'

'I think Madeleine Franks introduced us.' North noticed that the dealer had started to fiddle with a small gold signet ring on the little finger of his left hand. 'That was before she married Sigi. It was at a dinner party in New York. Sigi was keen to get into publishing, and my gallery was pioneering glossy, coffee-table illustrated catalogues. The production costs were too high for the gallery to justify and we needed a wider market. Sigi was offering instant distribution. It was a marriage made in heaven.'

'But it ended in an acrimonious divorce, if I may extend the parallel,' suggested Young.

'Well, yes, there were recriminations. Sigi handled all the finances and you could say he was one of the innovators when it came to imaginative accounting. I wish I'd never met him.'

'And when was the last time you saw him?'

'He was at Christie's about two weeks ago. He was examining a Stendhal, and when I spotted him I left.'

'And can you tell me what your movements were the day before yesterday?'

'I spent the morning here, preparing for the Jackson Pollock exhibition. Then I had lunch at Wilton's.'

'And after lunch?'

'I went to the Lords to put in some shooting practice.'

For the first time, Young looked puzzled. However, North could not tell whether it was the fact that Hardington had been at the Lords, or that he had been shooting, which had taken him by surprise. The Earl explained. 'I'm supposed to be captain of the Lords team for the Vizaniagram Trophy this year. It's an annual competition between the Lords and the Commons held at Bisley. I only do a little stalking in Scotland occasionally, so I need to brush up on my target shooting. There's a rifle range under the Lords, and that's where I spent part of the afternoon the day before yesterday.'

'What time did you arrive?'

'About threeish, I suppose. I was probably there for an hour.'

'And after that?'

'I came back to the gallery and then went around the corner to a reception at the National Gallery.'

'But you didn't see St Oliver on the day of the murder?'

'Definitely not. I rarely go into the Lords, and he's one of the reasons why. Anyway, there are more than seven hundred other hereditary peers to protect the nation's interests.'

'I understand that when Truscott & Sweeting crashed, you were one of the casualties.'

'That's a fair description,' agreed Hardington. 'He really screwed me, metaphorically speaking. I haven't had anything to do with him for a very long time.'

'But you were once friends?'

'He was never a close friend,' corrected the Earl.

'But you went to his parties at Stanton Harcourt,' replied the detective.

'You're very well informed,' he conceded, speaking deliberately slowly and cautiously. 'Yes, I went to Sigi's parties, but in those days I went to a lot of others, too. Don't get carried away with the idea that we had much more than a business deal and a few acquaintances in common. That was the sum of it.'

'Please don't think me impertinent,' said the detective, 'but did the losses you suffered as a result of Truscott & Sweeting leave you, er, financially embarrassed?'

'Not really,' mused Hardington. 'It was more than I'd bargained for, because Sigi had never told me the limit of his exposure. The problem was the U-boat libel case. Sigi was determined to defend the case, and the jury awarded record damages against us. Our author, who was a penniless academic, had virtually nothing, so we had to pay the lot. In retrospect, we should have settled as soon as the submarine captain had issued his writ. We could have got off very lightly then, but Sigi seemed so sure. We'd already had the *Himmler Diaries* fiasco, and this proved the last straw.'

'And were you bitter about the way St Oliver had run the company?'

'Not enough to kill him, if that's what you mean,' answered the peer. 'I shan't shed any tears over him, but he wasn't worth killing. Anyway, he wasn't entirely to blame for what happened to T & S.'

'Who was then?'

'It was that idiot Bill Staveley who authenticated the wretched *Diaries*, and what about Dick Hexton? He financed the U-boat captain to bring his libel action. If he hadn't stuck his oar in, the man could never have sued us.'

'Perhaps you could enlarge on how the, er, Duke of Hexton comes into this,' invited the detective.

'From what I've been told, Richard Hexton under-wrote the submariner's libel case. When a foreigner tries to bring a libel action in the High Court, the defendants usually try to obtain an order for security of their costs. It's to stop plaintiffs who lose from disappearing after the verdict. If they don't have any assets in England they have to lodge a whacking great sum with the Court. It's a useful deterrent. Sigi had calculated that this old man in Canada could never raise the money, but somehow a mysterious benefac-tor materialized in London and stood as surety. My information is that this individual was Hexton.'

'Why would he do that?' queried Young. From what he could recall from the gossip columns, Hexton was a middle-aged man best known for his collection of vintage racing cars. His house was open to the public and he was a regular of the Brighton rally, driving an exhibit from his museum.

'I have no idea. But he must have hated Sigi with a vengeance. I hardly know him.'

'But you're sure Hexton was the person behind the case?'

'Not *certain*, but pretty sure. The court documents were supposed to be confidential, but Sigi told me that he'd been tipped off that Hexton was the person who came up with the security.'

'He didn't tell you why he thought Hexton had done it?'

'No. If a plaintiff has a particularly good case, I suppose someone might take a gamble for a share of the damages, but that didn't happen here.'

'How do you know?' pressed Young.

'I was one of the signatures on the cheque. All the damages went to SSAFA, the services charity. None of it could have gone to Hexton without me knowing.'

'And what was the risk to Hexton?'

'If the U-boat skipper had lost, he would have been liable to pay all our costs, which were around a hundred thousand pounds in those days. I don't remember the exact figures, but Hexton would have had to pay for a sizeable chunk of that. Enough to hurt, anyway.'

'So Hexton must have hated St Oliver enough to risk backing an old Nazi,' murmured the detective, 'and with absolutely no obvious reward.'

Hardington nodded in agreement. 'The risk was really quite high. We hoped that the old boy would peg out before the case came to trial. If that had happened, Hexton would have had to pay his own side's costs, and that was a fair amount too.'

Young made a further note in his pad. 'And apart from Staveley and Hexton, can you think of anyone else who would have been keen to see St Oliver dead?'

'Isn't that enough?' smiled the peer, who was on his

feet and striding towards the door.

On the way to the City, in the back of the Ford, Young turned to the MP. 'They're an odd lot, these Lords, aren't they?'

'There's nothing odd about Hardington,' retorted North. 'He's entirely normal compared to some of the hereditary peers. What about the Sixth Earl of Stradbroke? He's an Australian, and his coat of arms is a kangaroo sitting on the john. That's quite colourful, as peers go.'

'It's what they call lifestyle, not colour, I meant,' said the detective. 'Anyway,' he challenged, 'you've been holding out on me again. What's this shooting gallery under the House of Lords?'

North swallowed hard. 'The Lords and Commons Shooting Club have a rifle range directly under the Lords. It's run by one of the police officers in the Members' Lobby in the Commons.'

'And you have to book in and out, so Hardington's times can be verified?' demanded Young.

'I'm not a member, but I think so. Any Member can join the club and use it, but I think you have to book in. I'll find out. But the crucial thing is that the entrance to the range is just off the Not Content Lobby, under the stairs that lead up to the Press Room.'

Young groaned audibly. 'And therefore opposite the Earl Marshal's Room. I remember it. Why didn't you say something? So Hardington had access to the murder scene?'

North nodded. 'What could I have said without accusing him? I hadn't really thought about the door under the stairs until he mentioned the range. Anyway, if he is the murderer, he would hardly have volunteered the information that he had been there.'

'But if you're right, and there's a written record of his visit to the range, he might have assumed that we knew already,' pointed out the detective. 'He is most definitely a suspect. St Oliver lost him a fortune, the dimensions of which he was deliberately vague about, and he was conveniently on the scene. In addition, he didn't sign in for his daily attendance allowance. Now isn't that rather curious? Who turns down tax-free dosh?'

North winced. 'Your theory depends on Hardington being very short of cash, but he doesn't look close to ruin to me. Indeed, he may not have registered for his attendance allowance for the very simple reason that he's already loaded.'

The DCI was sceptical. 'I think he failed to sign on because he hoped that his presence in the Lords that day would go unnoticed. Why didn't he go into the chamber, with the show of the decade underway, standing room only?'

'He's not political,' said North. 'He's never had any interest in politics. He probably didn't even know what the debate was about. Ask him about the temperature in Vail or Aspen, or the time of high tide at Lyford Cay, and he could tell you, but he probably doesn't even know who the Leader of the Lords is. The only subject he's ever expressed even the remotest concern about is hunting. He used to hunt twice a week but he's probably given that up now.'

By deft driving, Shawcross brought the car to a halt outside a large modern block in Leadenhall Street. 'Simons & Simons are on the fifth floor,' he said. 'Mr David Simons was expecting you ten minutes ago.'

North and the DCI gave their names to the receptionist in the lobby and made their way up to the fifth floor. As they stepped out of the lift David Simons was waiting for them, and he introduced himself with a firm handshake and a frown. 'We'll use the conference room,' he announced, leading them down a passage adjacent to the firm's entrance hall and waiting area.

Simons was not quite what North had been expecting. In his mind's eye he had visualized an establishment figure, perhaps one of those formidable lawyers like Lord Goodman or Sir David Napley, ever ready to protect the vulnerable reputations of important clients under threat. Instead, although David Simons was probably the right age, approaching retirement, his crumpled clothes betrayed no sign of a wealthy and influential clientele, and his harassed demeanour had more than a hint of a man under pressure, perhaps under siege.

He showed them into a panelled boardroom and enquired brusquely if they wanted coffee. Both visitors declined. 'A wise decision, gentlemen,' said the solicitor, wasting no time. 'I have here a statement from Susan St Oliver concerning His Lordship. She is anxious that there should be no misunderstanding concerning the religious ceremony she underwent in Italy recently. Under British law, they were not strictly husband and wife. If you have any questions, I would be very pleased to put them to her, but she feels that the ordeal she experienced yesterday was quite enough.'

'Surely her ordeal was the day before yesterday,' corrected the DCI.

'She was referring to her interview with you, which she found very harrowing. My instructions are that she is unwilling to see you again.'

Young considered the solicitor's remarks and read the sheet of headed notepaper he had been handed. It was a formal declaration that hereafter Susan Jane Mackay wished to be known as Susan St Oliver, and that she was the Common Law wife of Sigismund Rose, First Baron St Oliver. 'Is she also a beneficiary in his will?' he asked.

'I can confirm that she is the beneficiary of a trust created by His Lordship's will for his children. She has a lifetime interest in certain assets but the principal beneficiaries are the children, if any.'

'When was the will drawn up?' asked the detective.

'Six weeks ago,' replied Simons.

'And did St Oliver have any children in mind?'

'I understand that Susan St Oliver is expecting a baby.'

To the MP's relief, Young forebore to ask the solicitor about the identity of the baby's father. 'Nobody else stands to gain from St Oliver's will?'

'Apart from the executor and trustees, who will

receive minimal remuneration, that's all, unless other claimants appear.'

'What other claimants?'

'The will does not identify any single child by name so any of his offspring could qualify as beneficiaries, including those born out of wedlock, or St Oliver's children by adoption.'

'Did he adopt any?' asked the DCI.

'Not that I am aware of, but I've only been His Lordship's legal adviser since he regained his liberty.'

'And what assets will the trust have? St Oliver was only recently made a criminal bankrupt.'

'My client's bankruptcy was discharged quite a time ago,' said Simons. 'And although the will was drawn up relatively recently, the trust has been in existence for some years. As the accountants say, he'd been bankrupt but not bust. There's a difference.'

'What is the trust's value, then?' demanded the detective.

'I have no idea,' replied Simons smoothly. 'It is administered by a firm of lawyers in Bermuda and I don't have access to their working papers. I can only say that there will not be any estate duty liability in this country.'

'One final question,' announced the DCI. 'I would like to know who Susan St Oliver had lunch with on the day her husband was murdered, and I'd like a detailed schedule of her movements that afternoon. She told me she went shopping, but I need to know exactly where she went, and at what times as accurately as possible. She mentioned that she had lunch at Harvey Nichols. I need to know whether that was before or after the building was evacuated in the bombscare.'

Simons agreed to request the information. 'Am I to conclude from your question that my client is a suspect in the investigation?'

'You may conclude what you like, Mr Simons, but this is standard procedure in an inquiry of this kind. We have to eliminate Susan St Oliver and this is routine. Or perhaps you know of someone who might have wished to harm St Oliver?'

'I know of no one,' said the solicitor, rising to his feet. 'But I'll let you have this information as quickly as possible.'

In the lift on the way down to the ground floor, the DCI was gloomy. 'That was a complete waste of time. What a supercilious shit.'

North was more optimistic. 'At least we know for sure that the lovely Susie isn't really Lady St Oliver.'

Chapter Six

The Duke

As the unmarked police car headed down the Boltons towards Tregunter Road, North finished off his monologue about dukes, the highest of the five ranks of hereditary peerages. He had started, at Young's request, by quoting the College of Arms, on the exact status of the Aga Khan. 'His Royal Highness is regarded as a direct descendent of God. Dukes take precedence.

'There are twenty-four dukes in the House of Lords, of whom five are royal dukes. Andy was the last duke to be created, when he married Fergie, and Prince Charles was made the Duke of Cornwall when the Queen succeeded to the throne. The last non-royal dukedom was created in 1874. According to the librarian in the Commons, there have been less than five hundred dukes during the past six and a half centuries.'

'Any other useless trivia?' asked the detective, rhetorically.

'The Duke of Atholl is the only man in Britain permitted to run a private army, and dukes never wind their own watches,' offered North.

'So who does? A manservant? Let's skip the history lesson,' growled Young. 'Just let me know why the Duke of Hexton should have tried to ruin St Oliver. There's no obvious connection between them.'

'His Grace,' corrected the MP quietly. 'Was he the only duke in the Lords the day before yesterday?'

'Three others. Westminster, Roxburghe and Leinster. Know 'em?'

'Gerald Westminster I know,' acknowledged North. 'He used to command a tank in the TA. Very decent bloke, and very good to the Tory Party in Chester. I got to know him on summer exercises in Germany.'

'And what about our duke?'

'He started life as a photographer and married a model. He went to Eton and Exeter University, and now he runs a motor museum.'

'He was a photographer?' queried Young. 'That's an odd sort of job for a duke, isn't it?'

'You show your prejudices so obviously,' censured North.

'Prejudices? What prejudices? Police officers aren't allowed to hold prejudices any more. Black, white, lesbian, straight, handicapped or whatever, it's all the same these days.'

'And what about inverted snobbery, then?' countered the MP.

'What the hell's that?' demanded the detective. 'Snob, I definitely am not.'

'Inverted snobbery,' repeated North. 'You think being a photographer is the sole preserve of the working class . . . Terry Donovan and David Bailey.'

'Christ, you talk a lot of balls sometimes,' muttered Young. 'Haven't you got anything more on Hexton?' he asked, obviously disappointed by North's superficial pen-portrait.

'You're caught in a time-warp,' accused the MP. 'The dukes of *Kind Hearts and Coronets* are a dying breed, literally. They went with the Ealing comedies. Hexton has his motor museum and that's not so unusual these days,' said North. 'Peers have to make a living too. Alexander Hesketh used to make motorbikes on his estate at Easton Neston, and dozens of stately homes take in paying-guests these days.'

'Don't blame the DCI for being class-conscious,' said Shawcross, as he pulled the car into the kerb outside a large, semi-detached white stucco house, a Range Rover parked in what had been a small front garden. 'He likes his Lords to be known for something. He made John Lucan's reputation, but before him he'd only heard of sandwiches, cardigans and wellingtons.' Young ignored the comment and strode towards the front door which was opened almost instantly by a tall, eye-catching redhead in a thin cotton skirt.

'Hi, I'm Caro Hexton,' she smiled. 'Richard's in his study. Can I get you some coffee . . . or perhaps tea?'

'No thanks,' replied the DCI, answering for his two companions. 'We shan't be staying long. Just a couple of routine questions.' They followed the Duchess to the end of the long narrow hall, and admired the collection of marine prints on the walls. As they approached the end a door opened, and the Duke was framed in the doorway.

'How do you do?' he said. 'I'm Richard Hexton. Do come in.' He was wearing faded blue jeans and a cashmere sweater over a denim sports shirt. His hair was light brown, with faint blond streaks, and he wore rather battered suede Guccis. North judged that he looked much younger than forty-eight, the age given in *Debrett's*. He shook hands with his guests and waved them to an armchair and a sofa. He took his seat behind a large partner's desk, and the door was closed discreetly but firmly by the Duchess. As she made her exit she said, 'Please excuse me, but I'm looking after the children today. Give me a shout if you want anything. I'll be in the kitchen.'

'You want to see me about St Oliver?' asked the Duke, glancing at his wristwatch, a chunky steel and silver Rolex. A self-winder, mused North.

'That's right,' said Young. 'We are investigating his murder and I understand that you knew him. I also see that you were in the Lords on the day in question so we'd like your help to eliminate you from our enquiries.'

'Enquire and eliminate away,' invited the peer.

'Can you tell me the nature of your relationship with the dead man?'

'There was no relationship, as such,' replied Hexton. 'I never met him, but what I knew of him I didn't like.'

'What was the cause of your dislike?'

'It's personal. But I can assure you I had absolutely

nothing to do with his death. It wasn't a minute too soon, in my opinion, but I know less than zero about what happened on the day of the murder.'

'What time did you arrive in the Lords the day before yesterday?'

'I was there at eleven for a meeting of the Tourism Committee to hear Edward Montagu. Then I had a working lunch at the National Trust, and I was back for the start of Questions, at two-thirty.'

'Did you see St Oliver in the chamber?'

'Yes, I saw him, but I didn't speak to him. I never have.'

'Perhaps we can deal with this antipathy you have, or rather had, for him,' said the detective. 'This is a murder investigation, so there can't be any personal or private confidences involved. You have a duty to tell me all you know, and you may be sure that I will respect the sensitivity of any information you give me. But I must know. Do you understand?'

'It's not a matter that I should care to have circulated,' said Hexton cautiously. 'I hated St Oliver because he ruined the life of a great friend of mine.'

'And who was that?'

'Leander Byng. She was at a secretarial college, the one we called the Ox and Cow, when I was up at Oxford doing my postgraduate at St Antony's. She died of an overdose.'

'And why did you blame St Oliver for her death?'

'Because he introduced her to drugs. When I first met her she never even smoked. Then she started spending time with that creep, and the next thing was, she's dead. She'd be alive now if he'd left her alone. He was completely amoral, and corrupted lots of others too. That's not an accusation I'd make lightly, believe me. If ever somebody deserved to die violently, it was him, but I didn't kill him.'

'Were you in love with Leander?' asked the DCI quietly.

'That's none of your business,' said the Duke softly. 'Murder inquiry or not, that's out of bounds.'

'How did you meet her?' persisted the detective.

'When I was up at Oxford I spent most of my spare time taking photographs. She was absolutely stunning and when we first met, at one of the May balls, she agreed to sit for me. She was a natural model and could have been a superstar on the catwalk. We met . . . I liked her, but she died. That's it.'

'I see,' said Young. 'Why did you blame St Oliver for her death, and not Jonathan Aldworth. Wasn't he the person who found her?'

'Jonti had nothing to do with her death. Believe me, I took the trouble to find out. He's just a stupid prat, one of plenty whose life has been ruined by St Oliver. Just look at the man. He still can't walk properly, and how do you think he smashed himself up? He drove into a tree on his way back to Oxford from one of St Oliver's parties. St Oliver should never have allowed him to get into such a state in the first place, and he certainly shouldn't have let him drive. It was absolutely criminal. Jonti only became an addict after six months of continuous agony in the Radcliffe Infirmary. He's not to blame for Leander, it's St Oliver.'

'Is it true that you tried to ruin him?' asked the detective.

'How do you mean?' countered the Duke.

'I understand you helped finance a libel action against Truscott & Sweeting.'

'You have been busy, haven't you?' admired the Duke. 'Yes, I helped poor old Otto Schwemmer. He had a good case and he deserved to win. St Oliver was too arrogant and used every device to prevent the case from reaching court. But I made sure he was right royally screwed, as they say.'

'So you put up the money for him?'

Hexton nodded. 'All I did was provide a guarantee to the court for Schwemmer's costs. Without it, as a plaintiff resident abroad, he couldn't have continued the case. That would have been a grotesque injustice, and St Oliver would have escaped scot-free.'

'And how did you hear about Schwemmer's need for the security?'

'I happened to know one of the solicitors working on the case. He mentioned, quite by chance, that St Oliver was about to wriggle off a hook that could prove fatal to him and his business. That's all I needed to hear.'

'Did you consider that others might be affected by the collapse of Trustcott & Sweeting?'

'Only St Oliver's cronies. If the company had been properly managed, it would have survived Otto's libel action. In fact it was a pack of cards, and the crash would have happened sooner or later anyway. If you have any doubt, read the Price Waterhouse report . . .

It's absolutely damning. You could say that by being the catalyst I saved St Oliver's investors from a much bigger fraud later. You ask them. They don't blame me, they blame St Oliver.'

'Who particularly have you got in mind?'

'Charles Hardington springs to mind. He lost a packet, but he's never said a word to me about the Schwemmer case.'

'But does he know you were behind it?'

The Duke shrugged. 'You know, and presumably you've only been investigating St Oliver for the past twenty-four hours. Sure, CD knows.'

'And your motivation was to take revenge for Leander?'

'I can't think of a better one, but it's not something I would care to have broadcast around, if you know what I mean. My anger's long gone.'

'So you didn't kill St Oliver that afternoon?'

'Is that an accusation? No way.'

'And do you know who did?'

'No idea. But I wouldn't put it past Jonti. Or Leander's father.'

'Who's he?' asked Young, perhaps a little too sharply.

'You don't know? Then I'm not sure I should tell you.' For the first time the Duke looked ill at ease. 'I suppose you're bound to find out anyway. He's Michael Byng.'

Young noted the name on his pad. 'Any other reason to think he might be involved?'

The Duke shook his head. 'Frankly, I doubt he is.

He's a devout Catholic ... A Knight of Malta and all that, but if there is anyone who has a damn good reason for killing St Oliver, it's Leander's father. I'm not saying he did kill him, I'm merely answering your question. There're probably plenty of others too. Is that all, gentlemen?'

There was silence as the three visitors left the building. On the doorstep, Hexton mumbled a goodbye and closed the front door.

'So who the hell is Michael Byng?' asked North. 'I've never heard of him.'

'He's on my list of people in the Lords that afternoon. Unless I'm very much mistaken, he's one of the librarians. I think we ought to pay him a visit. And what about your nice junkie friend Jonti? He never said anything about his accident happening after one of St Oliver's parties, did he? That's a good motive for murder, being turned into a cripple and a doper.'

The MP made a face of disapproval. 'It's a longshot.'

'And then we have Hardington again. Why hasn't he ever said anything to Hexton about the Schwemmer case? By backing the U-boat skipper Hexton started St Oliver on the path to ruin, and didn't do much for Hardington's bank balance. Either Hexton is cleverer than I give him credit for, or he doesn't know that Hardington stood as guarantor for the company's bank account. That's another motive.'

'Who's next?' asked North as they walked to the car.

'Lord Staveley, at the Oxford & Cambridge Club, but don't change the subject. You didn't tell me that Hexton was at Oxford.'

'I didn't know he was. St Antony's is a graduate college. It doesn't take undergraduates.'

'So despite their age difference, Hexton and Aldworth were both studying at the same university, at the same time, and they both knew Leander.'

'And then Michael Byng?' suggested the MP. He was uncomfortable about the prospect of Jonti Aldworth and Richard Hexton being involved in a murder. He was also irritated that he had not realized the Oxford connection.

'I've arranged to see Lady Gresham at her room in the Lords this afternoon after Questions. Then we'll see Byng. What did you think of His Grace?'

'With a beautiful wife like that I don't suppose he's pining for Leander Byng any more,' observed the MP.

'Whatever the likelihood, he had access and he has a motive. That makes him a suspect.'

'But obviously not a very good one,' remarked North. 'Otherwise you would have asked him for the clothes he was wearing on the afternoon of the murder so they could be examined.'

'It's not quite as simple as that,' replied the DCI. 'I need to have some evidence to back up the request, in case there's a refusal and I need a warrant.'

'So why did Aldworth receive the heavy treatment, and not His Grace? Is this an example of a viscount being discriminated against in favour of a duke?' grinned North.

Young jutted his chin. 'Aldworth lied, and drugs have been found in his flat. That's more than enough reason to seize his clothes for forensic analysis.

Christ, we've nothing against Hexton. He's admitted to having got his revenge against St Oliver. As a murder suspect, he's not in the same league as Aldworth or even Hardington. The fact is, even Strelets looks better at the moment. I know when to be cautious, and this is just such a moment to exercise a little discretion.'

'I can hardly believe this is the same DCI Young speaking,' said North. 'Do you know, I really think you expected to find him in his scarlet and ermine.'

'If you weren't here at the personal request of the Lord Chancellor, I'd be tempted into a display of injudicious conduct right now,' warned the detective, as North tried to suppress a broadening smile. 'Let's deal with Staveley,' he suggested. 'How did he become a Lord?'

'He's one of the leading historians of our times,' said North. 'And as he's about the only one who isn't a Marxist he was given a peerage by Mrs Thatcher. He and Hugh Thomas are her favourite academics. He's written several big books on the Reformation and was in the Secret Service during the war. He's also something of a German scholar.'

'How did he get mixed up with St Oliver?'

'No idea. My edition of *Who's Who* doesn't relate that particular episode in his life. All I can tell you is that he's fond of publicity and he's not taken very seriously at High Table since the *Himmler Diaries* episode. Now I think he spends most of his time writing cranky letters to *The Times*.'

In less than twenty minutes the car moved out of

the fast-flowing traffic of Pall Mall and came to a
halt outside 71 Pall Mall, the home of the combined
universities. 'Go easy on the *Himmler Diaries*,'
advised the MP. 'He's probably rather sensitive on the
subject.' Young nodded and together they climbed
the six broad steps and entered the club's porch where
a liveried porter asked for the name of their host.
Implicit was the acceptance that neither man had
been an Oxbridge student. Perhaps neither had been
a university man at all. 'His Lordship is in the morning room, at the top of the stairs,' intoned the porter,
turning to answer a telephone in his booth.

The two men walked through a second set of double
doors and made their way up a magnificently carved
staircase. At the top the hunched figure of Lord Staveley was waiting for them. He was stooped so that
the coat of his grey suit appeared too large for his
frame, and his face was a mass of contours, deeply
lined as though he was a schoolmaster who had spent
a lifetime peering in poor candlelight at bad hand-
writing. He still had plenty of unkempt, white hair,
which contrasted with the heavy black rims of his
glasses.

'Bad business, bad business,' he muttered as he
appeared to ignore Young's outstretched hand and
motioned them into a large drawing room, the walls
dominated by huge portraits of obscure academics.
'May I offer you a sherry?' suggested Staveley, peering
over the thick lenses of his spectacles. Both North
and the detective declined the invitation.

'I don't want to take up too much of your time, sir,'

said Young with uncharacteristic deference. 'I am here
to enquire into the death of Lord St Oliver, who was,
I understand, a friend of yours.'

Staveley said nothing, evidently waiting for the
detective to finish his question.

'I believe you were in the Lords the day before
yesterday afternoon, when Lord St Oliver met his
death, and I am anxious to know what you have to
tell us,' continued Young.

'I didn't kill Sigi, if that's what you think,' said
Staveley with surprising firmness. His voice was
stronger than his hunched body and arthritic hands.
'I can't say I was distraught to hear of his passing,
but that's that. The man was ghastly . . . an absolute
shocker.'

'But you knew him quite well,' protested Young
gently. 'Weren't you his business partner?'

'Certainly not,' replied the peer with a frown. 'Sigi
once published a book of mine, and I think he cheated
me. He also bullied me into giving him an opinion on
some German documents, and then quite misrep-
resented what I had said. The man was really dreadful. No decency whatever.'

'Can you tell me how he cheated you?' enquired
the detective.

'It was really too simple,' said the peer, as he
cleaned his spectacles on his tie. 'He agreed to publish
an account I had written at the end of the war about
the liberation of Berlin. I knew there was a real
market for the book, particularly in America, but he
tricked me out of the US rights. Whenever I asked

for a royalty statement it never showed my American sales. Sigi had changed the terms of our contract and had pocketed all the worldwide income of the book.'

'And what did you do about it?'

'I consulted my solicitors and Sigi agreed to settle the matter but he never paid me in full. I didn't really want it to go to court and it was in my interests to accept his settlement terms. Unfortunately, it tied me even closer to him and when he sought my opinion on some German material he behaved appallingly.'

'These were the *Himmler Diaries*?'

'As you well know, Mr Young, they were no such thing. I merely gave an opinion about the language used, which was quite authentic in my judgement, but Sigi twisted what I had said. He announced that I had authenticated the contents of the so-called Diaries, but that was completely untrue. The language was right, and that's all I said. I'm not qualified to examine paper and ink, or assess the age of a document. I had warned him about the Mussolini Diaries. They had been written by a grandmother who used an old stock of notepads and aged them by cooking them in an oven. On that occasion *The Sunday Times* offered a quarter of a million pounds for the rights to publish them. Of course, they were bogus.'

'And clearly you hold St Oliver responsible for what happened to you?'

'Who else?' demanded Staveley. 'All he was interested in was the money. He has no concept of intellectual integrity and he ruined me. I still had a decent part of my career before me, but Sigi's misrepresentations finished that completely. He was entirely without scruples. He even had the cheek to suggest that the forgeries would sell just as well. He was quite devoid of principles.'

'Can you tell me how you met him?' asked Young.

'We were introduced when he was "studying" at Ruskin College. He flattered me, and told me that he intended to start a publishing house in London. I suppose in retrospect he offered me rather more than was justified for my book, but that's hindsight. Anyway, I scarcely knew him, but later he was to cling like a limpet. He was always after me to endorse books and recommend authors. That was the trouble with Sigi. Once he had caught you in his web he drew you in. I wish I had never met him.'

'Can you recall who introduced you?'

'Most certainly. I think she's very embarrassed about it now, but it was Liz Gresham.'

'Is that the Baroness Gresham?'

'Of course,' replied the academic. 'I'm sure she'd prefer to forget about Sigi too, but it would be more difficult for her.'

'How's that?' enquired the detective.

The old academic hesitated. 'She really took a liking to Sigi when they were up at Ruskin. I think she felt sorry for him. Or vice versa. They were both very left, very committed Socialists in those days. Either way, she was able to shake him off, but I never was. That bloody man ruined me.'

The DCI considered what he had heard. 'What did you know about St Oliver before you met him?'

'Originally? Absolutely nothing.'

'And what do you know about his origins now?'

'I have read that he's an immigrant... That he came to England as a penniless refugee after the war, and made his fortune. I seem to recall that he's probably Latvian or Estonian... I don't recall.'

'So you had no contact with him in Germany immediately after the war?'

'Certainly not. I was an intelligence officer until I was demobbed in December 1945, and then I worked for the Control Commission before returning to my Oxford college. I am afraid I know very little about Sigi, except that he is fluent in German, but can't read *Heutdeutsch*.'

'What were your duties in the Control Commission?'

'Partly the administration of Münster. I also helped set up some of the denazification panels.'

'Do the names Rosenbaum or Orobinsky mean anything to you?'

'Not a thing,' said the octogenarian, squinting through his glasses as though he had missed part of the conversation. Either he was genuinely mystified by the detective's line of questions or he was a damn good actor, thought North.

'And on the day of the murder... Can you tell me where you were before you arrived at the Lords?' asked Young, abandoning his previous tack.

'I spent the morning here, in a committee meeting. We are to have yet another tedious vote about granting women membership of the club, and then I lunched at Lords. I rarely attend these days, but I wanted to hear the war crimes debate.'

'Did you have lunch alone?' asked the detective.

'No. I joined that young pilot Inchkenneth and Lord Liverpool. Interesting fellow . . . A descendent of the Prime Minister. Not a university man, I believe — neither of them is actually — but that's the joy of the Lords. Always full of interesting chaps from all walks of life. Do you know, I once sat down at a club table next to a London bus driver. It takes all sorts.'

Young noted the names of Inchkenneth and Liverpool in his notebook. 'Do you know what time you went into the chamber?'

'I'm sorry. I did a little work in the library at the Lords on a bibliography I am preparing, and then I took my seat for the debate. I think Noel Annan was on his feet when I went in. I stayed in the chamber until I heard about Sigi's death.'

'And you had absolutely no contact with him the day before yesterday?'

'None whatever.'

'Can you recall when you last saw or spoke to him?'

'Chief Inspector, I'm in my eighty-first year and my memory is not what it was. But I haven't seen that charlatan for more than two years. I'd bet on it. Nor did I kill him. You have my word.'

'Have you any idea who might have?'

'Perhaps creditors, perhaps an enraged husband, I really don't know. He had plenty of enemies, and I was among them, but I didn't kill him.'

The DCI took his leave and thanked the historian for his co-operation. As he accompanied the MP down the stairs, he was crestfallen. 'He's too old and too short to have been the murderer. That's not our man. But I wish I'd known St Oliver had been to Oxford.'

'It's probably not significant,' replied North. 'Ruskin runs a lot of short courses, especially during the long vacation. I don't think St Oliver ever went through a full university term at Oxford.'

'But what about Lady Gresham? That's the second time her name has come up,' said the detective.

'Obviously they must have had some relationship. Do you know her?'

'I don't, but I'm sure Rendell does. When he was a minister she was his opposite number in the Lords.'

'Find out what you can, and see if anything is known about Byng. We'll see them this afternoon, but I've another engagement first. Perhaps we can meet in the Central Lobby, around four? We'll drop you off at the Commons.' It was hardly a question, and North recognized from the DCI's tone that he should not delve too deeply into how Young was going to spend the intervening few hours.

The appointment the DCI had to keep was with Tony de Gruyt of the Security Service. They met in the saloon bar of the Albert, not two hundred yards from New Scotland Yard. When Young arrived, he saw de Gruyt in an alcove of the deserted saloon bar, sipping a vodka and tonic. Taped music from the far side of the bar made it unlikely their conversation would be overheard.

'So you got my message,' opened the detective.

'It's not convenient,' replied the MI5 officer. 'You

can't suddenly ring and demand meetings. Why didn't you simply call my colleague? That was the arrangement. Leaving instructions on my vodaphone is not what I call proper liaison.'

'Nor is telling me porky pies,' said Young fiercely. 'I'm not some plod to be crapped on. This is a murder inquiry and I intend to identify St Oliver's murderer and get a conviction. All this "Box 500" shit may impress the funnies, but I have a job of work to do. When I ask a straight question, I require proper answers. We're supposed to be on the same side, but I'm beginning to wonder.'

'Calm down,' urged de Gruyt. 'Tell me what the problem is and if I can help I will. Now, what is all this about?'

'Firstly, Bicton is a fucking liar. You may have been a little economical with the truth, but your so-called legal adviser is eligible for a Nobel Prize. How long have you known that St Oliver was a war criminal named Orobinsky who was wanted by the Soviets?'

De Gruyt took a sip of his drink. 'Strelets, eh?'

'Yeah, Strelets. How come a Russian journalist knows far more about this case than I do?'

'He's not entirely reliable, I'm afraid,' said de Gruyt.

'Not reliable? He's got more credibility in my book than either of you two bastards. Now, are you going to tell me the truth about St Oliver or not? If you don't, I'll have to consider my options.'

'I don't think you'll find the Assistant Commissioner Crime very receptive to your complaints, whatever they might be,' ventured the case officer.

'Who said anything about the ACC?' asked Young. 'I'm reporting directly to the Lord Chancellor, and the trouble with him is he doesn't entirely trust me. In fact, he has so little faith in me that he's given me a sort of minder. There's a really nosy MP called Philip North who watches everything I do. But I have to watch him, too, because he's a sight too close to several lobby correspondents. Do you catch my drift?'

De Gruyt nodded bleakly. 'What have you told him about our meeting yesterday? Everything that was said was classified. I thought you understood that.'

'Genuine secrets are classified,' agreed North. 'Bullshit isn't. North knows I've been talking to the funnies, but he doesn't know I've been given the run-around. He knows nothing about an attempt to pervert the course of justice . . . yet.'

'Philip North must know nothing of this,' said de Gruyt. 'Mr Bicton may not have told you everything, but that is no reason to leak classified information to the press. That would be a breach of the Official Secrets Act.'

'So you would prosecute an MP, would you? You'd persuade a jury that it was in the public interest to lie to the officer leading a murder inquiry? I can hardly wait.'

'There's no need for all this,' said the MI5 officer smoothly. 'Let's not have threats and counter-threats. They aren't getting us anywhere. Ask me what you want to know and I'll see what I can do.'

Young shook his head. 'That's not good enough. I want answers now. We'll start with Strelets. Who is he?'

'He's a Soviet intelligence officer. Probably holds the rank of major. You've been told all that.'

'It's what you haven't told me that's the most interesting part. Why does he know so much about St Oliver?'

'Because we suspect that St Oliver was put under pressure by the KGB when he established contact with his mother.'

'Are you saying that St Oliver was a Russian spy?'

'Not exactly. We know St Oliver had meetings with Soviet intelligence personnel but we don't know the substance of what took place. As you were told, St Oliver declined to help us so we were powerless to intervene. In any event, St Oliver has not had access to classified information so he probably wasn't a spy. If he was, he was of no great consequence.'

'But wasn't he working for intelligence when he was at Bodmin and that RAF station in Scotland? Who was he working for then? Strelets says he was training agents to be dropped into Russia.'

'Our best guess is that St Oliver was compromised by one of his students who probably named him in a subsequent confession. I'm afraid that most of the allied agents who were infiltrated into the Baltic countries after the war were rounded up by the Soviets. We have to assume that St Oliver was betrayed by one of them, and that when he began corresponding with his mother the attention of the Soviets was drawn to him again.'

'So you admit St Oliver was working for British Intelligence?'

'I've never denied it,' said de Gruyt casually. 'He

was one of a dozen or so language teachers. It so happened that some of his students were intelligence officers.'

'And when he was employed, was it known that the identity of Rosenbaum had been adopted?'

'That I can't answer, because I don't know. Frankly, I doubt it. If I had been Rosenbaum, and I had acquired a new identity to conceal my past, I wouldn't be very inclined to declare myself to the victorious allies.'

'So when, exactly, did you learn that Rosenbaum was not quite what he seemed?'

'I really don't know,' replied the MI5 officer easily. 'I inherited the file from my predecessor and the first mention of the name Orobinsky is in the context of a memorandum from the Northern Department of the Foreign Office. It contained a list of suspected war criminals who, according to the Soviets, had taken refuge in Britain. I'm not sure what happened next, but there may have been an administrative foul-up because I can't see that the three names of Orobinsky, Rosenbaum and St Oliver were connected again until quite recently.'

'But your suspicion is that the KGB traced the person who was sending letters to Orobinsky's mother and discovered that he had changed his name to Rosenbaum. So when the KGB met Rosenbaum they were in a position to blackmail him, probably on three accounts. Firstly because he was a war criminal, and secondly because he had acquired British nationality under a false identity, and thirdly because he wanted an exit visa for his mother. Am I right?'

'It's speculation, but all the ingredients are there, I grant you,' conceded de Gruyt.

'Then why did Bicton deny to me that St Oliver had been named as a war criminal by the Soviets?'

'Because he wasn't. As I recall, you asked if St Oliver's name had appeared on any Soviet list. The answer is that it didn't. What Mr Bicton told you was the truth.'

'But not the whole truth,' complained the DCI. 'He might have said that St Oliver's *other* names had been on the list. That would have been closer to the truth. He might even have told me that Rosenbaum was actually a war criminal called Yacov Orobinsky, but he didn't. I want to know why.'

'There's no sinister reason,' said de Gruyt smoothly, as he took another sip of his vodka. 'None of this is relevant to your investigation and we have responded to every one of your questions. We've hidden nothing, although I agree we did not volunteer every last item in the file. You wouldn't expect us to.'

'Yes, I would,' replied the DCI. 'This is a murder inquiry and you have a duty to co-operate fully. How do you know St Oliver's past has nothing to do with his murder? I am the only person qualified to make that judgement, and I can only do so when I'm in possession of all the facts. If you know something else that's relevant, you'd better come clean now.'

De Gruyt put his hands up in mock surrender. 'St Oliver was a scumbag ... A low-life. I can't say categorically that his past had nothing to do with his death, but I doubt it. There's nothing in his personal file to even give the merest hint of a motive. I expect you'll find a wandering psychopath was responsible.'

'But you don't know that, do you?' challenged the detective. 'That's for me to judge. On the face of it, Strelets is in the frame. He knows all about St Oliver's past, he definitely had a motive, and he was on the scene.'

'If Strelets had a motive, it was to keep St Oliver alive,' retorted the case officer. 'Alive he was a ticking time-bomb, a really useful piece of propaganda. Imagine . . . An English milord who was really a Nazi murderer. The British establishment clasping to its bosom a man convicted of monstrous atrocities. He's not much value as dead meat. Don't you have a better suspect?'

'There's a Doorkeeper named Cox who has all the physical attributes the murderer requires. He's old but as strong as an ox. An ex-Marine and ex-Special Boat Section.'

'And why did he do it?'

'That's where the theory collapses,' admitted Young. 'Plenty of access to the scene, but no obvious motive. He may have been acting as a hitman, or even have been in league with someone else.'

'Who has the best motive for killing St Oliver?'

'I've just been to see a duke with a reasonable motive, and I'm to interview a librarian in the Lords with an excellent one. St Oliver allegedly raped his daughter, who then committed suicide. That's a terrific reason for cutting someone's throat.'

'Christ,' murmured de Gruyt. 'You don't mean Michael Byng, do you?'

'You know him?'

'Know him? I only worked for him for ten years. He was my director.'

Chapter Seven

The Life Peeress

North had agreed to meet Young at four in the Central Lobby so he could attend the interview with the daunting Liz Gresham, but he was intercepted by one of the tail-coated Badge Messengers almost as soon as he entered the Members' Lobby of the Commons. He was handed a sheaf of familiar pink slips, all telephone messages from the message board, just as a group of hovering correspondents bunched themselves around him. They fell upon him as eager rubber-necked spectators congregated at the site of a motorway pile-up, or hungry animals closed in on a potential meal.

'How well do you know Lord Aldworth?' asked one. 'Is it true that he's to be charged with St Oliver's murder?' demanded another. The old Press Association veteran came close to the borderline of taste, as usual, with his impish accusation: 'Have you ruled yourself out as a suspect?'

'I'm merely acting as an observer and a parliamentary adviser to the police,' replied North. 'You'll have to direct your questions to them. I have no statement to make yet,' he added as he glanced at his messages, a time-honoured method of demonstrating to members of the lobby that their attention was unwelcome. To press their luck was not only against the lobby's own rules, but would invite a complaint and perhaps a rebuke from the lobby's own respected leader, the ITN Channel 4 News correspondent.

One of the message flimsies in particular caught North's eye, and according to the time printed on the top it was more than two hours old. The Lord High Chancellor of Great Britain wanted to see him urgently at his office in the Lords, and he was to make contact without delay. It was a summons that he had half expected, and when he was ushered into the palatial office on the committee floor of the Lords, beside the Victoria Tower, he realized the encounter was going to be a difficult one. As he headed towards the Central Lobby he was intercepted at the heavy double doors by Tony Rendell, who was deep in conversation with another former member of the Commons, Lord Harmar-Nicholls. As former Members of the Lower House they were entitled to use the facilities of the Commons, and these two in particular were often to be seen chatting to old colleagues in the Members' Lobby.

'Just the man!' exclaimed North, as he spotted the immaculate Rendell. 'What can you tell me about a librarian in the Lords called Michael Byng?'

'Has he replaced me as your suspect for Sigi's murderer?' asked Rendell with a languid smile, as Harmar-Nicholls waved farewell and headed predictably towards the tea room.

'Apparently Sigi was less than pleasant to his daughter, so there's a possible motive,' answered North. 'The police want me to check him out before they see him.'

'Does that detective know what he's doing?' queried the peer disdainfully. 'I wasn't hugely impressed, if you know what I mean. No wonder he couldn't catch Lucan.'

North deliberately ignored the comment about Lucan, but wondered how Rendell knew Young had been on that murder hunt. Or had it simply been a lucky guess?

'What can you tell me about Byng?' he asked.

'Absolutely nothing. I rarely use the library. But what is Sigi supposed to have done to his girl?'

'Rape, apparently. Then she committed suicide . . . But keep it to yourself. Anyway, the police are interested. Coincidentally, her boyfriend was Richard Hexton.'

'Sigi was quite an operator,' mused Rendell, with a slight tinge of admiration in his voice. 'He rather made a habit of behaving badly to women. Do you remember what he did to Alastair Inchkenneth's wife? She was in the Priory for months after Sigi's revelations. He's really no loss. Perhaps it's just as well there's a policeman of his calibre in charge.'

North murmured his thanks to Rendell and

continued on his way to the Lords, feeling a little
disloyal for not having supported Young. However,
there was a kernel of truth in Rendell's barbs. They
were no closer to identifying the murderer, and the
DCI was plainly insensitive to the need for diplomacy.
As he made his way towards the Lords' Lobby he tried
to recall the Inchkenneth saga. It had been some
years ago, not long after Alastair had married Sarah.
They were both quite a few years younger than North,
perhaps in their early thirties, and according to a
book written by a former *Daily Mirror* crime reporter,
Sarah's father had been a notorious East End villain.
The story had been a sensation, and Sarah had suffered a miscarriage and a breakdown. Now the story
was coming back to him ... Sigi had published the
book. North wondered whether Inchkenneth also had
a motive, and whether he had been around the Lords
at the time of the murder. As he had known the
Marquess for most of his life, he wondered too if he
should pass on Rendell's comment to DCI Young.

'Do come in, Philip,' growled the Lord Chancellor in
his Highlands brogue as the MP was ushered straight
into the magnificent high-ceilinged room by a member
of the private office who closed the door firmly as
he left, hesitating only momentarily in case he was
required to take notes.

'I see from this morning's papers that young Jonathan Aldworth has been arrested on a drugs charge,
and there is some connection with St Oliver. Is he
the murderer?'

It was hardly a question the MP had expected to

hear from the Lord Chancellor, the guardian of the nation's judiciary, despite his reputation for plain speaking. The MP took a leather armchair close to the desk, as the peer started to light a small cigar, signally failing to offer him one from the silver box on the desk.

'The police are waiting for a forensic report but Aldworth's not the best candidate.' North wondered whether he should also express some doubts about the validity of the drugs charge, but thought better of it.

'Have the police any idea about what they're doing?' demanded the peer as he examined the end of his cigar.

'So far we've interviewed a viscount, a duke, a life peer, a disclaimed peer and a belted earl. And that's not counting a widow who may or may not have married a baron, and a bishop and a Doorkeeper.'

'This is no time for levity,' murmured the Lord Chancellor with a perceptible groan. 'Are the police close to identifying and arresting the killer?'

'Not that I can tell,' replied North.

'It really can't be a Doorkeeper. That would be terribly bad for morale,' observed the older man drily as he took a puff. When he had been a circuit judge his sense of humour had been hugely popular. 'Can we expect an arrest?'

'Not imminently,' said the MP tactfully. 'Perhaps you ought to talk to the police yourself. I may not be privy to everything that's going on here.'

The Lord Chancellor glanced up from his desk. 'You

are supposed to be my eyes and ears. Mr Speaker says you're capable, and that's what I expect. From what have you been excluded?'

North refrained from commenting that he could hardly know the answer to the question. 'I know there's some Special Branch interest. The detective leading the inquiry was given a briefing but I wasn't invited along.'

'That's intolerable,' said the Scot. 'I'll deal with that at once. Is there some foreign involvement here? Why should Special Branch be part of this?'

'The man we knew as Sigi St Oliver did not start life as Sigi Rose, or even Sigi Rosenbaum, as most of us had generally supposed,' explained North. 'We think his real name was Yacov Orobinsky, and that he may have been a war criminal.'

The Lord Chancellor took a deep breath. 'And there was I thinking Sigi was nothing more than a crook and a shit. Having listened to almost nothing but war crimes for the past week or so, I can't say I have an appetite for much more on that particular topic.'

'According to the TASS correspondent who happened to be in the press gallery, and is also from Lithuania, Sigi was a murderer in his own right . . . A member of an SS police battalion composed of Lithuanians.'

'But wasn't he Jewish?' protested the peer.

'Apparently that didn't affect his sense of self-preservation,' replied North. 'He wore a Nazi uniform and then adopted the identity of a Jewish refugee as soon as it became convenient to do so.'

'So when he came to England he wasn't a victim of oppression, but rather its instrument,' said the Lord Chancellor with solemnity, flicking ash from the lapel of his double-breasted grey suit.

'Special Branch are obviously interested in Sigi, and probably in the TASS journalist too.'

The Lord Chancellor took another draw on his cigar as he pondered the situation. 'Who's the duke?'

'Richard Hexton,' answered the MP.

'Harmless,' remarked the peer. 'If the viscount's Aldworth, who's the earl?'

'Charles Hardington.'

The Lord Chancellor shrugged his shoulders. 'Believe anything of him. Who else do the police suspect?'

'Tony Rendell hasn't much of an alibi, but not much of a motive either, and they're due to see Liz Gresham very soon, and then a librarian named Byng.'

'Michael Byng? He's all right. What's wrong with him? He's a damn good librarian and something of a military historian, I believe. He wrote that rather good book on the Salerno mutiny. He got all his information from my predecessor, Elwyn Jones, who was on the court-martial. It'd be a shame to lose him.'

'Apparently Sigi behaved rather badly towards his daughter,' said North cautiously, with some understatement.

'Have you told them to go easy on Liz? She'd make an excellent psychopath but I pity the police who arrest her. Who's the representative of the Lords Spiritual on the list of suspects?'

'Donnington. Actually, he's a retired bishop.'

'Come to think of it, I remember seeing him in the chamber that day. He was the one who made a completely unnecessary fuss in the Sunday trading debate in the last session. It was on one of the very rare occasions Their Lordships demanded that the Clerk at the Table read the Standing Order on Asperity of Speech. That shut him up. A life sentence for him would be purgatory for his fellow prisoners . . . A cruel and unusual punishment if ever there was one.'

North nodded his agreement. 'He's been a little evasive about St Oliver but we can't quite figure out the reason. He was in Germany after the war, and it's possible they may have met in a refugee camp.'

'I hadn't realized Sigi had enjoyed such a wide circle of friends,' commented the Lord Chancellor. 'A Church of England bishop is really too improbable.'

'I don't think they were friends – quite the opposite – but Donnington is not very forthcoming. He may know rather more than he pretends about Sigi's past.'

'And these other members of the Lords. Were they simply on the scene or are they also suspects?'

'Rendell's biography of Sir Desmond Morton was published by Sigi, and it seems that Sigi cheated most of his authors. Of course he ruined old Bill Staveley, and he was applying pressure to Jonathan Aldworth. That gives them good motives.'

'Staveley's a silly old fool who ruined himself,' said the peer. 'He just loves to see his name in the papers but I can hardly picture him sneaking up behind Sigi and cutting his throat.'

'Nor can I, but none of them really seem very likely,' admitted North.

The Lord Chancellor rose to his feet, indicating that the interview was at an end. 'You keep an eye on these policemen and keep me informed. I don't want to hear about the Birmingham six, the Guildford four, the Tottenham two and have the Lords loner added to a very disagreeable list. Make sure they get the right man. If there's any more nonsense about secret briefings, let me know and I'll sort it out. Just remind them that this is a royal palace and I'm in charge here. Any mischief and they'll answer to me, not the Commissioner. What time are you seeing Liz Gresham?'

'In half an hour,' replied North, reminding himself not to make any of the suggested remarks to the DCI.

The Lord Chancellor frowned. 'Good luck. You'll need it.'

Before returning to the Central Lobby, the MP walked the length of the Committee Corridor and wondered about the Marquess of Inchkenneth. He had obviously been in the Lords on the day of the murder, because Staveley had mentioned him as one of his luncheon companions. But had he stayed in the Lords for the rest of the afternoon? If he asked the police whether his name was on their list, Young would want to know why. He thought of asking Alastair himself, fairly confident that although he might regard the Lords as a sort of comfortable London club, he had never spoken in the chamber. The chances are, he would have left immediately after lunch. He thought of checking with Eddie Liverpool, but that seemed too much like spying on friends. Finally, after much hesitation, he placed a call from one of the Members' telephone boxes in the Upper Waiting Hall to a helicopter charter company based in a small office in Lower Sloane Street. The telephone was answered by Alastair Inchkenneth.

'Alastair, it's Phil North.'

'How's the legislator?' asked the younger man.

'Running a murder investigation, if you must know. Tell me this, because I've got to be brief. Did you have lunch with Bill Staveley the day before yesterday?'

'That silly old fart, the historian? Sort of,' he agreed with some reluctance. 'I was having lunch with Eddie Liverpool at the Lords and Staveley plonked himself down beside us. Why do you ask?'

The MP overlooked the question. 'Did you go into the chamber afterwards?'

'Yes, I did. I'm planning my maiden speech, you know. I've talked it over with Tom Galbraith and Ivan Brabazon. They're both old hands and they say it's essential I start to listen to a few debates before I give my maiden. Good advice, eh?'

'That's fine,' replied North. 'But were you in the chamber when Sigi St Oliver was murdered?'

The telephone line went silent. After a few moments, the Marquess said, 'So, Phil, you're trying to shop me to the law?'

'Of course not,' answered North coldly. 'I just need to know if you were there, that's all. The police already know.'

'Well, I didn't kill the old bastard, if that's what

you think. So you can sod off.' Now the line was disconnected. Was Alastair really a murderer? North doubted it, but at the back of his mind there was a tiny feeling of insecurity. He realized that whoever was responsible, he didn't want the person to be one of his friends. An acquaintance, maybe, but not a friend like Alastair or Jonti. He was still preoccupied by the swift termination of his conversation with Alastair Inchkenneth when he met Young and Shawcross in the Central Lobby.

'Sorry to have kept you waiting, gentlemen,' said the MP. 'I was detained briefly by the Lord Chancellor.'

'Name-dropper,' accused the senior detective. 'Not detained during Her Majesty's pleasure, I trust.'

'He wanted an update. I told him that the inquiry was progressing normally.'

'There's nothing normal about this investigation,' retorted the DCI. 'St Oliver's bank manager has referred us to that solicitor again, so we're making an application to a High Court judge in chambers this afternoon for a warrant.'

'What about Byng? I'm told there's nothing extraordinary about him. He's regarded as a good librarian and something of a military historian.'

'He's had a book published?' queried the detective.

'Apparently, rather a good account of the mutiny at the Salerno landings in 1944. I haven't read it myself, but the Lord Chancellor knew about it.'

'And was it published by St Oliver?' demanded the DCI, as they walked towards the Lords' Lobby.

North kicked himself. He had been so distracted by Alastair Inchkenneth that he had failed to make the most elementary check. As a member of the Commons he was unable to go into the Lords Library, but he could have used the highly efficient reference section in the Oriel Room, as the Commons library was known, to see who had published Byng. 'I'll find out this evening,' promised North.

'I don't know how long this warrant will take, so we'll see Byng first thing in the morning,' declared Young as the trio made their way past the Cholmondeley Room on the lower level, having been acknowledged twice on the route by passing Doorkeepers.

'I ought to warn you,' said North, 'that Liz Gresham has a certain reputation. It's what used to be called an unfortunate manner, if you get my drift. She's, well, volatile. How you handle her is up to you, but she tends to blow up like Vesuvius.'

'I'm not taking any bloody nonsense from a woman, Lady or no Lady,' replied Young. 'This is a murder inquiry, not a croquet match.'

'Suit yourself, but she's very touchy. Even her own side treat her with kid gloves.'

'And I suppose you're going to tell me why she's so touchy? No man in her life?'

North raised an eyebrow at the detective's remark. 'She was married once, years ago, before she entered politics. God knows what became of her husband. Then she had a child much later, and it was always assumed that St Oliver had been the father, but if the pathologist is right, it looks as though all the

178

gossip has been a little wide of the mark. Anyway, she's quite a tyrant and she's never said who the father was.'

'And how long ago was this tryst?'

'Ages. When she was up at Ruskin.'

'Anything else?'

'She's very highly thought of in the Labour Party. Came into national politics through local government in Yorkshire, and has shadowed Trade and Industry and Overseas Development. Not nearly as good look-ing as Tessa Blackstone, but intellectually they're on a par.' North considered adding something about her not suffering fools gladly, but he reckoned that he had said enough. They approached a series of office doorways, and he knocked on the door marked 'Baron-ess Gresham of Lyford'.

'Come in!' barked a voice, and the three introduced themselves to the life peeress, a rather large woman with half-moon glasses dangling from a cord around her neck. She was in her mid-sixties, North guessed, and still had handsome features. Her hair was streaked grey and tied firmly and unfashionably in a bun at the back of her head. She wore a plain red suit but no jewellery, and had kicked off her shoes. Her desk, dominated by a large brass lamp with a green shade, was piled high with documents and a map. 'I can only spare you a short time as I've got an Overseas Development committee in half an hour, but I'm sure that will be plenty,' she said firmly. 'Tell me what you want to know.'

'We're inquiring into the death of Lord St Oliver,'

opened the DCI, 'and Mr North here is representing the Lord Chancellor, under whose authority I am conducting this investigation. Can you first of all confirm that you were in the chamber on the afternoon St Oliver was killed?'

There was a long pause while the Baroness gazed into the middle distance. 'Before we begin,' she said slowly, 'I should like to know how I stand. Am I a witness or a suspect? Is this conversation privileged?'

'It is a preliminary, informal conversation to determine whether a formal statement is required. I expect Mr North can clarify the technical point about privilege, but you will notice that I have not given you a caution.'

Before North could interject, the Baroness had embarked on an assault. 'This is no technical point,' she said heatedly. 'You may think this place is some mausoleum, but we do serious work here, and what takes place within the precincts is privileged. Make no mistake about that.'

'Perhaps we should begin again,' said a rather startled DCI. Despite North's warning, her aggression had taken him by surprise. 'I'm here to seek your help, not make accusations. I have no reason to believe you need legal representation, but I am anxious to establish the nature of your relationship with the deceased.'

North held his breath, anticipating an explosion, but none came. The Baroness had a well-earned reputation for a fiery temper, and the DCI was either being deliberately obtuse, or somewhat indelicate. Both were provocative.

'Very well, Chief Inspector, I'll take your word for it. As you have doubtless already heard, I was once close to Lord St Oliver, long before either he or I came to this place. In those days I knew him as Sigi Rose, a man who pioneered food storage and gave the working man the opportunity to eat green vegetables all the year round. He was an idealist and we were both committed to the Labour Party. He was creating jobs and reclaiming derelict land, and I was a grammar school teacher and a county councillor. I suppose I knew him as well as anybody, and I recognized his talent and ambition. He made and lost several fortunes over the years, but he always treated his workforce well.

'When he came down to London, he changed. I won't say he was corrupted by what he found here, but he lost his ideology. The Rolls-Razor crash was the start of the trouble, but he was mixing with the wrong crowd. We parted company, both politically and socially, and then by one of those strange quirks in life I was elevated to the peerage just four years ago, only to find Sigi on the same benches. He'd had a rough time of it, and much of his misfortune was of his own making, I won't deny. But he never lost his sparkle. He was an extraordinarily gifted individual, and you should not make the mistake of classifying him as some old lag.'

'Thank you for putting us in the picture,' said the detective. 'Perhaps you could now tell me if you were in the chamber on the afternoon in question?'

'You know perfectly well I was,' she retorted. 'I gave my details to a police officer at the time.'

'Very well. You must understand that I have to double-check all our information. A murder inquiry has to be completely thorough.'

'I know that,' replied the Baroness sharply.

'Thank you. Now, can you tell me what contact you had with Lord St Oliver on the day of his death?'

'We didn't speak,' admitted the peeress. 'I saw him in his place in the chamber after Questions, but we didn't speak to each other.'

'Does that mean that you never spoke to each other, or just on that afternoon?' asked Young, seizing his opportunity.

'I haven't spoken to Sigi since I've been in the House,' said Lady Gresham cautiously. 'Oh, I may have exchanged a couple of words when I first arrived, but I always had to be careful not to compromise the Party. In spite of everything that happened to him, he insisted on taking the Labour whip. As a front bench spokesman, I had to be very careful. I therefore decided to adopt a policy of indifference towards him.'

'So apart from a few words when you came to the Lords, you haven't spoken to St Oliver at all.'

'That's right,' agreed the Baroness. 'But the fact that we had gone our separate ways does not mean I wished him ill, and I certainly did not kill him.'

'Indeed,' accepted the DCI. 'However, I have to investigate every avenue. I regret that there is no way of seeking clarification of this point delicately, so I must ask you bluntly. What exactly was the nature of your relationship with St Oliver when you first met him . . .?'

'It's irrelevant to—'

'Let me be the judge of what is, or is not relevant, please,' interrupted the detective. 'As I was saying, what was the nature of your relationship?'

'Since you appear to know already, it would be fruitless to deny that we had an affair when he came up to Oxford. It didn't last long, and I quickly regretted it.'

'And you are not resentful of the way he treated you?'

'Don't be impertinent!' scolded Gresham.

'I am trying to establish whether you, or anybody else perhaps acting in what they believed were your interests, might have had an interest in his death,' said the CID man, evidently exasperated.

'That is tantamount to an accusation of murder, and I resent it,' said Gresham, her colour rising. 'I will not listen to this nonsense.'

'I understand your indignation,' said Young untruthfully, 'but I have a duty to look at everything. Can you tell me if there is anybody you know who would have wanted him dead?'

'I have no idea what his financial arrangements were like, but I suppose he might have been killed for his money.'

'But he was a bankrupt,' pointed out Young.

'Agreed. But Sigi was nothing if not shrewd. He would have salted away some cash. If you look hard enough I expect you'll find a Swiss bank account or an offshore company or two. Sigi was like that. Always taking precautions.'

'Is there anyone in particular whom you regarded as Sigi's enemy?'

'There was someone behind his famous libel case, but I expect you've researched all that,' recalled the Baroness. 'Whoever that was hated him enough to dredge up some ancient dispute and destroy his publishing empire. Perhaps it was one of his creditors. Quite a few lost money when Truscott & Sweeting went under.'

'In my experience there has to be a stronger motive than revenge over lost money to compel someone to commit murder. Most of St Oliver's victims are, by my standards anyway, really very wealthy people . . . The sort who regard losing a few thousand pounds on an investment as an occupational hazard. But in the absence of other motives, we have to look at what might be termed his private life.'

'Then you'll have to look elsewhere, I'm afraid, Chief Inspector. I know absolutely nothing about that side of him.'

'But surely you do?' said the detective gently. 'What can you tell me about his wife, for example?'

'No idea. When I knew Sigi he was between wives. He had just ditched his first wife, who was American and went off back to the States, and Madeleine hadn't got her claws into him yet.'

'His first wife is dead, and his second is somewhere in France at the moment,' said Young. 'What about Maisie?'

'Is that his third wife?' she asked without interest. 'I did not concern myself with any of that.'

The detective accepted defeat. 'Very well. Let's turn to St Oliver himself. You knew him as Sigismund Rose. Is that correct?'

'That's true,' agreed Gresham. 'Of course, I knew that he'd adopted that name. Anyone could tell from his accent that he was from Eastern Europe.'

'Did you know his true name?'

'I think he may have mentioned having anglicized his name, so I suppose it was something like Rosen. There's nothing wrong in that.'

'Of course. But did he ever tell you what it had been?'

'No, I don't think he did . . . and I certainly didn't presume to ask.'

'And even today you don't know?'

'I've already told you,' said the Baroness, slightly irritated. 'Perhaps you'd like to enlighten me.'

'He changed his name from Rosenbaum to Rose by deed poll. It was all perfectly legal,' said the detective. 'Now perhaps we can turn to your movements on the afternoon in question. Can you tell me where you were?'

'I attended a lunch at the Indian High Commission, and I was in my place in the chamber in time for Questions.'

'And did you stay in the chamber continuously?'

'I may have slipped out briefly during the debate to the Earl Marshal's Room, but I wasn't gone long.'

'Did you see anyone else there?'

'I remember Lady Masham was there, and Sally Oppenheim may have popped in. I don't recall.

185

They're both very assiduous attenders.'

'Can you tell me what route you took from your seat to the Earl Marshal's Room?'

'It's only across the Not Content Lobby from the Opposition benches, so I usually go through one of the two side doors. I don't recall which one, exactly.'

'But your most direct route would have taken you through the doorway where Lord St Oliver died,' remarked Young.

Lady Gresham nodded in agreement. 'I must have come and gone well before the murder, because I saw no sign of him.'

'Did you see anyone else on your way?'

'Apart from my colleagues in the Earl Marshal's Room? There may have been some visitors on their way up to the gallery. I'm not sure.'

'Have you ever come across a Soviet journalist called Viktor Strelets? He was in the Press Gallery that afternoon.'

'Definitely not,' she replied.

The DCI glanced at his watch. 'I'm sorry to have detained you, and thank you for your co-operation. It really is appreciated, I do assure you.'

'I can't say it was a pleasure, Chief Inspector. Thinking of Sigi brings back some painful memories. It's not easy. And that afternoon is still something of a blur. I am sorry.'

The three made their exit and walked slowly back towards the Central Lobby. 'She's very vague if she has the brainpower you claim,' commented the DCI. 'But she's hardly a candidate for a crime of passion.'

'I thought you handled her very well, if I may say so,' said the MP. 'You even avoided asking her about the paternity of her child. Congratulations.'

'The fact is, Phil, that I'm reaching certain conclusions about this case. When you've eliminated virtually all of the options, you're left with some very limited choices. That's the stage we've reached. I think the end is in sight.'

'So you know the murderer?' gasped North.

'I'm not positive, but I think we're almost there. That's all I'm going to say. I've got to get to the Strand in a hurry, and I'd be grateful if you could find out about Byng's publisher. That may just be the key to all this.'

'So it's Byng?' said North with relief. 'But why are you delaying the interview until tomorrow? Surely he ought to be seen as quickly as possible?'

'Byng isn't going anywhere, you may be sure of that,' replied Young with a knowing look. 'But there are other considerations here. We have to handle this one very carefully. He can't make a move outside this building without us knowing. I'll see you in the morning, but in the meantime, not a word to the Lord Chancellor, please.'

'That's fine,' agreed North, 'but perhaps I can ask a favour. Earlier this afternoon I spoke to Alastair Inchkenneth, who had lunch with Staveley in the Lords on the day St Oliver was murdered. I think he may know something so perhaps he ought to be interviewed.'

'Staveley's not much of a suspect,' observed Young.

'Why trouble with Inchkenneth to corroborate a lunch appointment?'

'I wondered whether Inchkenneth might have had a motive, and now I'm sure he knows something. If he's not a suspect himself, he may be able to offer a clue. Can I borrow Mr Shawcross to talk to him?'

'You want to do this now?'

'Indulge me, Chief Inspector,' pleaded the MP.

'Be my guest. I'll drive myself to the law courts and the Inspector can pursue Lord Inchkenneth for you. Satisfied?'

Chapter Eight

The Marquess

North and Shawcross were being driven west, along the Embankment, in a black cab. As promised, DCI Young had gone alone to his meeting with the Crown Prosecution Service in the Strand, intent upon seizing all St Oliver's bank and financial records.

'I suppose "Inchkenneth" is one of your Lloyd George titles?' asked Shawcross, not disguising his contempt.

'Certainly not!' replied North. 'You're as bad as the chief. Alastair Inchkenneth's family goes back to before the Act of Union.'

'What does he do, apart from marry the daughter of a villain?'

'You are well informed,' conceded North, impressed. 'Is that a result of a telephone call to Criminal Intelligence or a lifetime of reading the *Mirror*?'

'I'm a *Guardian* man, myself,' said Shawcross. 'Those lads are famous at the Yard. They'll come unstuck eventually, even if one of the family marries some blue blood.'

'There you are again,' joked the MP. 'Another one of your prejudices has surfaced. What have you got against impoverished young men who go into the son-in-law business?'

'So that's what you call it,' said the Inspector. 'Doesn't he realize that his father-in-law is a hard nut? Now isn't that a strange turn of events, aristocrats marrying into the villainy? The Marquess's father-in-law did time, you know. GBH down the Mile End Road. His firm's kept the City Road nick in business for years. Made those south-of-the-river merchants like the Krays and the Richardsons look like kindergarten novices.'

'But Sarah's not part of all that,' said North. 'She's clever, pretty and, most importantly as far as Alastair is concerned, loaded.'

'So that's what counts, is it? Money and not breeding?'

'Listen to yourself,' chided North. 'You're as bad as Betty Kenward or Peter Townend. Alastair has expensive habits and he has indulged in too many fast women and slow racehorses. He plays polo in Julian Hipwood's team and runs a helicopter. That's a high-goal team with some of the best ponies in the country, and a fearfully expensive machine. By luck, or ill-fortune, he's also got an expensive house to maintain.'

'What's luck to do with it?' demanded Shawcross. 'He chose his wife.'

'But it was luck that he inherited the title. He's a twin, and he was born less than a minute before his brother. If it had been the other way round the title would have gone to his younger brother.'

'And what has he to do with any of this? As the chief said, Staveley's not in the frame. He's not a runner.'

'Then tell me what has suddenly persuaded him of Byng's guilt? Until Hexton mentioned his name you'd never heard of him. Now, in the space of a few hours, Byng's on the verge of being arrested. If he's really the murderer, why don't you go and arrest him now? Why is the chief so keen to go haring off for a warrant to look at St Oliver's accounts? Byng's probably in the Lords right now, and we must have been only a matter of a few hundred yards from where he works when we saw Lady Gresham. Her office is almost directly under the Lords Library. What's going on?'

'I don't know the full story, but the chief had another meeting with the funnies this afternoon,' admitted Shawcross. 'That's why I had to take you straight back to the Commons after seeing the Duke.'

'So MI5 have been involved, because of Strelets,' murmured North. 'I should have guessed.'

'The problem is, Byng used to work for the Security Service. The chief's man at Box only told him this afternoon. As well as obtaining a warrant to serve on St Oliver's solicitors and bank, he's applying for a search warrant for Byng's home. The plan is to wait for Byng to leave the Lords, and arrest him at home either late tonight or early tomorrow morning.'

'The Lords are sitting late tonight, and the Lords

Library staff remain on duty until the House adjourns. It could be any time.'

'The later the better is the theory. A forensic team are standing by to examine Byng's clothes. If the evidence is there, he'll be arrested as soon as he walks through the door. We know Byng was on duty on the day of the murder, and as an official he has unrestricted access to the Not Content Lobby. As for motive, Hexton and Aldworth have offered an excellent one, and all of that should add up to a warrant and maybe an arrest.'

'Which saves the embarrassment of an arrest in the Lords itself,' muttered North.

'The CPS says Byng doesn't have any immunity in the precincts of the Palace of Westminster, but it's still a little awkward, if you know what I mean. He'll be kept under surveillance from the moment he leaves tonight, and we'll pick him up as soon as the evidence materializes. There's also a complication with Box. Obviously they want to be in at the kill because of his past employment. So does the Branch.'

'That doesn't surprise me. Quite a few of the staff at Westminster are retired spooks. They often go for a job as a clerk.'

'So there are others like Byng? Ex-Box types working at the Commons?'

'I've no idea how many, but I know of at least three,' said the MP.

'And what can you tell me about Inchkenneth? How does he fit into all this? Make it quick, because we'll be there soon.'

'I don't think Alastair really knew about Sarah's family background until a *Mirror* crime reporter included it in a book about East End villains. It caused appalling problems for Alastair, mainly because his father-in-law had put up a lot of capital for his helicopter business. Sarah was expecting a baby at the time, and she lost it. Then she suffered terrible depression and went into a private bin. It was ghastly, and all because of some gratuitous comments which were nothing whatever to do with Sarah. She was devastated.

'The book itself was garbage, but the *Mirror* serialized it for a week. Worst of all, it was published by Sigi, who was entirely unrepentant. They already have a daughter, but if Alastair doesn't have a male heir, the title will die.'

'Why wouldn't it go to his brother?'

'He was killed in a hunting accident two years ago.'

'And when did you realize Inchkenneth might be a suspect?'

'When Staveley mentioned him as having lunched in the Lords that day. Alastair never goes near the place, partly because he can't bear to see St Oliver, so his appearance there was perhaps not entirely coincidental.'

'But you only told us about him after the chief had explained that Byng was our man. Does that mean you had intended to keep quiet?'

'I hope not,' replied North honestly. 'I called him to see why he had been there, and he gave me a reason. But then he put the telephone down on me. That's not like him. If he's not a suspect, it may be that he knows something.'

The taxi drew up outside a large house two-thirds

of the way up Lower Sloane Street, towards Sloane Square, and North paid off the driver. 'My treat,' he said to his companion. 'It's my idea, so I'll pay.'

At the entryphone North announced himself and a secretary buzzed the front door open and invited them up to the first floor where Inchkenneth ran his charter business. As the two men reached the landing halfway up, they encountered the Marquess. 'What the hell are you doing here, Philip?' he demanded, menacingly.

'He's here because I asked him to bring me here, sir,' intervened Shawcross. 'I'm Detective Inspector Shawcross of the Metropolitan Police and I'm seeking your help in a murder inquiry. May we come in?'

Inchkenneth bristled with rage. 'Is this to do with St Oliver?' he asked as he threw himself into a large reclining leather seat behind a long glass trestle table, leaving his two older visitors to sit on a pair of perspex chairs.

'This morning I interviewed Lord Staveley, who informed me that you had lunch with him at the House of Lords the day before yesterday, sir. Is that correct?'

Inchkenneth glanced at North, but the MP gave him no sign. 'That's quite true.'

'And can you tell me what you did after lunch?'

'I went into the chamber.'

'Can you tell me where you sat?'

'I sit on the cross-benches, which are just below the Bar of the House.'

'What time did you arrive in the chamber?'

'I'm not sure. Questions had been on for some time.'

'Very well. And what time did you leave?'

'After the murder. I wanted to go home to my wife.'

'And did you leave the chamber at any time in between?'

'No,' said Inchkenneth firmly.

'Did you see Lord St Oliver in the chamber?'

'Of course.'

'And did you speak to him?'

'No. I'm not in the habit of talking to filth.'

'So there was some animosity between the two of you?'

'Let's be entirely frank about this, Inspector. I hated St Oliver. He was a dangerous, meddling bastard who deserved to get his throat cut. I don't know who did it, but I applaud them, whoever was responsible. The man was a monster.'

'Did you kill him, sir?' asked Shawcross quietly.

'No, I did not,' replied the peer without hesitation.

'Do you know who did?'

'I'm not willing to answer that. I have my suspicions, but that's all.'

'Can you tell me the evidence upon which you base your suspicions?'

'Can you give me a good reason why I should?'

'Because it's your duty,' said the police officer simply.

'Noblesse oblige, eh?'

'No, it's nothing to do with your status,' said the detective. 'It's to do with citizenship. It is also a legal requirement. If I am satisfied you have information relevant to my enquiries, and you obstruct me, I can have you charged with a serious criminal offence. And please believe me, I won't hesitate to exercise my power of arrest if I consider it appropriate.'

The Marquess looked as though he had been chastened by the threat. 'I have no proof, you understand. But Charles Hardington has been having an affair with St Oliver's live-in floosie. I saw him in the Lords car-park a very short time after the murder, and he seemed in a hurry. I know he hadn't come out of the Peers' Entrance, because that's the way I came out of the building, so where had he been? I had the impression he had emerged from one of the inner cloisters.'

'So you think Lord Hardington may be the murderer?'

'It's possible,' shrugged Inchkenneth.

'And what makes you think he's having an affair with Lady St Oliver?'

'I once saw them having lunch together at Wilton's. There was no mistaking it. About a week later I was asked the same question by Ross Benson, the diary editor on the *Daily Express*.'

'Why did he ask you?' asked the detective, more out of curiosity. He had often wondered where the diary columnists found their snippets of gossip.

'He thought I might know. Sarah was organizing a charity ball for Mencap, and Charles's wife was on the committee. Benson assumed we were friends, and rang me. I told him I didn't know, but he wouldn't tell me where he'd heard the whisper. He's very well informed, you know.'

'So your theory is that Lord Hardington cut St Oliver's throat for love of Susie St Oliver?' concluded the detective.

'It's a little more complicated than that. I think Hardington was out to destroy St Oliver. His only interest in Susie was to spite St Oliver. Finally, I think he was driven to killing him, and I don't blame him.'

'And what was the motive compelling Hardington to do all of this?'

'That's easy,' said Inchkenneth. 'Hardington is skint. He's been fighting the banks for ages, but they've taken over his gallery and he's having to move out of his house in Eaton Terrace. He's about to be bankrupted.'

'But surely Lord Hardington is one of the richest men in England?' protested Shawcross. 'Isn't his part of Gloucestershire known as Hardingtonshire because he owns so much of it?'

'The estate owns it, not him. It's all in trust, and entailed. Hardington will never be completely broke, of course, and he'll continue to live in some style on the estate, but he'll have no cash. But more importantly, he'll have to give up the Lords.'

'But according to what I've heard, he doesn't go there very often anyway. It's not much of a sacrifice.'

'It's the humiliation, not the practical effect. No peer has been barred from the Lords since St Oliver went to gaol. It's ruin for Hardington, and all because St Oliver tricked him into standing as guarantor for the company's massive overdrafts. He stands to lose everything he has ever done on his own account, and the final insult is that St Oliver was attending the Lords every day as though nothing had happened. The gall of the man was breathtaking.'

'Put like that, I rather take your point,' agreed the detective. 'He has a right to be bitter, but no right to take the law into his own hands. But you have nothing more concrete than this vague feeling? Nothing really solid? I ask because we know Hardington was in the rifle range at the time of the murder, or rather he was supposed to be. For him to have slipped out of the range and up into the Not Content Lobby, at exactly the right moment, is leaving too much to chance. As you yourself said, sir, Hardington rarely attended the Lords. If he visited on that occasion with the intention of killing St Oliver, he must have done more than trusted to luck. How would he have known when St Oliver was leaving the chamber?'

'Suppose he had arranged to meet St Oliver?' suggested North.

'Alternatively, he might have seen St Oliver leave on one of the television monitors, or he might have had an accomplice.'

'Have you anyone in mind?' prompted Shawcross.

'Not me,' replied the Marquess. 'But what about one of the Doorkeepers?'

'Why do you say that?' asked Shawcross. 'Why would a Doorkeeper help a peer with a murder?'

'It's loyalty, Inspector. Quite a few of the Doorkeepers served in the forces with the peers. It's a tremendous bond between them.'

'And are you saying that Hardington served in a particular regiment?' asked the detective. 'That should be easy to check.'

'I can tell you right now,' answered North. 'I remember from when I looked him up in *Who's Who*. Hardington did a short service commission in the Royal Marines.'

'Which puts a certain Doorkeeper, ex-Sergeant Major Laurie Cox, in the frame,' acknowledged Shawcross under his breath. 'They would have served together.'

It was seven-thirty, and North had been up since the beginning of the *Farming Today* bulletin on Radio 4, much to Debbie's irritation.

He was up early in anticipation of a summons to Byng's interrogation. After his encounter with Alastair Inchkenneth the previous evening he had returned to the Commons alone, promising Inspector Shawcross that he would feign ignorance about the information he had imparted concerning the unexpected appearance of MI5 in the investigation and their interest in Strelets and Byng. The last vote, on a money resolution, had taken place at eleven-thirty, and unusually North had remained in the chamber for the adjournment debate in the hope that he would hear from Young before the House rose, but as he had made his way out through St Stephen's Entrance he had noticed that the Lords were still sitting. Whilst the Commons routinely continued past midnight, their Lordships generally preferred to end their deliberations at a more civilized hour, but that evening had been exceptional. It also meant that the Lords staff would be going home late, so North calculated that Byng's arrest would not happen until some time well after midnight, allowing for the librarian to travel home to Chalcot Crescent, off Primrose Hill. Shawcross had assured the MP that sophisticated precautions had been taken to keep Byng under continuous surveillance from the moment he stepped into one of the ordered cabs which ferried Parliament's officials to their beds.

North had slept badly, not so much because Debbie had been excessively frisky, but rather he had been troubled by the events of the past few hours. How was he to explain to the Lord Chancellor that a member of the Lords staff had been arrested, and he had been prevented from giving him advance notice? If news of Byng's previous employment reached the media the conspiracy theorists would have a field-day. He could see the banner headlines already: 'Spy Scandal in Lords' in the *Mail*, 'Toff topped by Spook' in the *Sun*, and probably plenty worse elsewhere. In North's experience members of the Cabinet didn't mind hostile stories in the tabloids. They just hated being caught by surprise. He had therefore listened to the first morning news bulletin on Radio 4 with some anxiety, in case he had really been shafted by Young and an announcement had been made concerning the arrest. Fortunately, there had been none, and North wondered what had happened. At ten to eight, the telephone rang.

'Good morning, Philip. I'd appreciate it if you could come over to the Commons.'

'You've made your arrest?' queried the MP with excitement.

'I'm afraid not,' replied the detective. 'Byng hanged himself late last night. I'm arranging a news blackout but it can only be temporary. I thought you ought to see for yourself and then have a word with your master.'

Chapter Nine

The Librarian

As North made his way up Great College Street towards the Commons, he was overcome by a sense of relief. The sun was breaking through the heavy morning clouds and the weather forecast was good. Suddenly all the anxiety he had felt over facing the Lord Chancellor had evaporated. Byng, the former MI5 man, had taken it upon himself to kill St Oliver. By all accounts, he had done everyone a favour, including St Oliver's grieving widow. Now, overcome by remorse, he had hanged himself. He was a mere officer of the House, not a Member, and that reduced the embarrassment quotient dramatically. In his haste and surprise North had neglected to ask the DCI where the librarian had chosen to kill himself, but provided it wasn't the chamber itself, he reasoned, it hardly mattered.

For a moment North caught himself wondering why he was so preoccupied with appearances. Did it really matter what the press said? Was his initial reaction an indication that, against his protests to the contrary, he really had joined the establishment and was therefore keen to protect its institutions from being undermined? Or was the solution more simple? He hadn't wanted any of his friends to be implicated in a murder, and in particular he felt slightly responsible for Jonti Aldworth, who was still languishing in custody, scheduled for a bail hearing that very morning, or Alastair Inchkenneth, who had already been put through enough trauma without having the police trample through his family's affairs. In contrast to the two young men, whom he had known for most of his life, there was the anonymous Byng, a man he had never met, whose death would probably go unremarked. His bloody despatch of St Oliver had not been the work of a psychopath who had wandered in off the street, thereby implying a grotesque breach of security in the Palace of Westminster, but rather the calculated act of a highly intelligent, strongly motivated individual who had every legitimate reason for being in the Not Content Lobby at the relevant moment. Christ, thought North, when you really think about it Byng's ideal. His suicide leaves everyone satisfied.

But as North loped up the steps to St Stephen's Entrance, past the two constables who gave him a surprised salutation, a feeling of doubt began to well up in his mind. *Was* Byng the murderer? Of course he was, he rebuked himself. The MP made his way across Westminster Hall, but was directed to the

Commons Library by a detective who was packing files into cardboard boxes. The police weren't wasting any time in getting their disappearing act underway, he thought. In less than two minutes North had taken the back staircase up to the deserted Members' Lobby and walked briskly up the Library Corridor. At the end, at the entrance to the Oriel Room, he found DCI Young.

'Good morning, Philip,' he said brightly. 'It seems Michael Byng hanged himself late last night. The only outstanding question is whether there was a leak and he discovered we were waiting for him at his home.'

North wondered whether this was an accusation, and hoped Shawcross would enlighten him if he had confessed his indiscretions of the previous evening to the DCI. 'Where did it happen?'

'In the furthest part of the library ... I gather it's called Room C. He was found early this morning by a cleaner. He was attached to a set of library steps in the military history section.'

'May I see?' asked North.

'Not much to see,' observed Young. 'The body's been taken for a post-mortem, and the scene of crime team are there at present. Once they're through you can cast your expert eye over the scene. Then you ought to inform the Lord Chancellor.'

Young led the way past a uniformed constable and through the double doors into the library. The two reception desks, usually manned by four librarians, all graduates with experience of fielding requests for help with research from MPs, were empty, and the two men turned left into the magnificent main library room which overlooked the Thames. On most days the long writing desks were occupied by Members, and the computer consoles and monitors were illuminated with teletext news and information from database services. At this hour of the morning, the room was utterly deserted. They walked silently past the empty chairs and moved into the second room, known as Room B. Whilst short, quiet exchanges were tolerated in the main room, this room was governed by a stricter regime and conversation was discouraged. It contained all the day's daily newspapers and half a dozen extremely comfortable leather armchairs grouped around a fireplace where MPs could close their eyes and concentrate without fear of interruption. The third room, Room C, was an inner sanctum where complete tranquillity prevailed and it was protected from even the slightest extraneous noise from Room B by a heavy oak door. This was a room in which there was never the slightest danger of a Member uttering any sound except, perhaps, a snore. It was not exactly cosy, with bookshelves rising to the ceiling on three walls, but it was quieter than the grave. Today, however, as North and the detective approached, there was a considerable commotion. To North, used only to MPs entering this hallowed chamber, the sight and sound of strangers talking to each other at quite normal voice levels appeared almost akin to sacrilege, as though a group of rowdy football supporters had invaded a sacred crypt, and the alien experience assaulted his senses. If the DCI was unaware of the contrast between Room C's usual atmosphere and the conditions prevailing that morning, he gave no sign of it.

'Byng was found here, halfway up these steps,' said Young, pointing to a library ladder lying on a plastic sheet laid over the carpet beside the shelves. Almost every inch of the wooden frame had been covered in metallic fingerprint dust, indicating that it had already been given a forensic examination. 'He had asphyxiated himself with what looks like a curtain sash from the Lords Library. We haven't spoken to the library staff yet but I'm informed by the constable responsible for security at this end of the building that the usual form is for the two main rooms to be tidied during each division, leaving this room untouched. A librarian checks the room when the House adjourns, and switches off the lights. It is then swept, dusted and the bins emptied by the cleaners at around seven in the morning. On this reckoning, Byng must have entered after the librarian had closed the room for the night, climbed the ladder and hanged himself. Sort of ironic, him being an author and this being the history section.

'The last division was at around eleven-thirty last night, and the adjournment debate went on for about twenty minutes, so I suppose the House rose slightly before midnight,' North recollected.

'The Lords went on later,' responded the DCI. 'They didn't adjourn until twelve-fifteen, so Byng waited until the library closed, and then slipped in here. The only puzzle is why he didn't do it in his own library. Any suggestions?'

North considered the situation for a moment.

'Maybe he wanted some peace. At least here he knew there was absolutely no danger of being disturbed. If he came in here before the Commons rose for the night he would almost certainly have been spotted by one of the librarians because the only access, as you can see, is through Room B.'

'But there are two entrances to Room B, aren't there?' noted the detective. 'He could either have walked into the main library, as we have done, and through Room A into Room B, or he could have come into Room B directly from the corridor outside.'

'That's right,' agreed the MP. 'If he came in through the Oriel Room, one of the librarians would have seen him. They may not have challenged him, as he was also a librarian, but it probably would have been a courtesy to give some explanation for his presence. The Commons librarians guard their premises just as jealously as their counterparts in the Lords.'

'Either way, we'll have a pretty exact time of death when the autopsy has been completed. The temperature in here is kept at a constant level so the pathologist will be quite accurate. His preliminary findings are some time after midnight, so that fits with what we already know. As soon as the library staff turn up we'll know some more.'

'There was no suicide note?' enquired North.

The DCI shook his head. 'It would have saved a lot of trouble if he had left a confession, but I expect the forensic team will come up with something. They've been working on his clothes all night.'

North concluded that Shawcross had said nothing

208

of their conversation the previous evening, and pretended to be surprised by the news. 'So you really intended to arrest Byng?'

'He had the motive and opportunity, which only leaves his inclination and the murder weapon. If St Oliver had raped my daughter and driven her to suicide, I think I might have cut his throat,' added Young. 'We were all ready for him last night, but he never went home. If we find the murder weapon there, it's game, set and match.'

'What else is known about him?' asked North as he glanced at the books on the shelf beside the ladder.

'Leander was his only child, and her death devastated him and his wife, who says that she has suffered from depression ever since. My officers told her the very minimum last night but she may have found a way of letting her husband know that the police were in the house. We can't be sure because she's in shock this morning. Frankly, I think she's a basket case. Her cupboards are full of Valium and she really cracked up when the news was broken to her this morning. She's in hospital now, and she can't be interviewed.'

'So you think she told him the police were waiting for him, and he realized the game was up?'

'It's a possibility. We had a WPC with her almost all the time, and we think we covered the telephone, but perhaps she had a mobile phone on the premises. On the other hand, he may simply have been overcome with remorse. It does happen.'

'So you think she knew her husband had killed St Oliver?'

'It's difficult to tell. Maybe he confided in her, maybe he didn't. A statement from her would be very helpful but we may have to wait some time for that, until the doctors give us the go-ahead.'

'There's one thing that bothers me,' murmured the MP. 'It's what the Duke of Hexton said. Although Byng was upset at his daughter's death, he was also a Knight of Malta. Catholics don't believe in suicide.'

'Religion is no obstacle for those determined to top themselves,' replied the DCI dismissively. 'You can take my word for it. Mortal sin or not, Catholics commit suicide.'

'Do they?' asked North. 'Really devout Catholics? It takes years of commitment to the faith to become a Knight of Malta. I'm not sure what the exact qualifications are, but they take the church's law fairly seriously.'

The detective looked sceptical. 'What are you trying to say? That Byng's death wasn't suicide?'

'Perhaps,' admitted North.

'On what evidence?' demanded Young.

'Not much, I admit,' conceded North. 'He was a devout Catholic, but we've covered that. Then there's this place; why did he come almost the entire length of the building to hang himself? Why not do the job in his own library? And what about the sash? You're sure it's from the Lords Library?'

'Positive,' said the detective. 'The uniformed officers spotted it at once and I've seen the window where it comes from. I really don't think we need a forensic comparison to prove it matches the one on the other side.'

'OK, but isn't that rather odd? Imagine, you've taken the decision to kill yourself. You remove a curtain sash from the Lords, and then you carry it out of the Lords, through the Inner Waiting Hall, into the Commons, past the Commons dining rooms, and into the Commons Library. On the way he'd have passed at least half a dozen interesting places to hang himself, including two cloakrooms where he'd be guaranteed privacy. But instead he goes into what is, for an official of the Lords, alien territory. Strictly speaking, he's out of bounds, and he walks calmly into the quietest room and hangs himself.'

'In the military history section,' added Young, obviously unconvinced by North's scenario. 'He may have decided to kill himself, come into the library for a final read of his favourite book, and then done the dirty deed. What's so odd about that?'

'I don't get it,' said North. 'Either this was a spontaneous episode, which is not supported by the presence of the sash from the Lords, or it was calculated. If it's the latter I can't see the logic behind it. I think you ought to dig a little further.'

The DCI threw his hands up. 'Dig *where*? There's nothing else here. We have a body, a ladder and a sash. All three will be subjected to the most detailed examination by the forensic scientists. What more do you want?'

'Let's try the books,' suggested the MP. 'Supposing

he came in here to look at a book he couldn't find in the Lords. It was your idea that he wanted to read something before he died. Can't you check the books to see which he handled?'

'Are you serious?' gasped the DCI. 'There must be ten thousand books in here!'

'Very well,' said North, casting his eye over the military history shelves. All the books in the immediate area were on the subject of the Second World War. 'What about dusting all the books in this bookcase in case Byng touched any of them?'

'I'll compromise,' said Young. 'We'll dust all the books that were within reach of the ladder. Does that satisfy you?'

'Entirely,' said North. 'And what do you want me to say to the Lord Chancellor?'

'Tell him that we have good reason to believe that Byng murdered St Oliver, and that a search is being conducted at his home for the murder weapon and for forensic evidence linking him to the scene of crime.'

'And what about Byng himself?'

'You can say that there will be an inquest and he can see the results of the post-mortem as soon as we have them. The preliminary findings will be ready this afternoon.'

'That's not what I meant,' explained the MP. 'What do I tell him about Byng the person? What do you know about his background?'

'Oh, I see,' said Young. 'He was fifty-nine, and had worked in the Lords for four years. No criminal record, retired senior civil servant, usual stuff.'

'Oh, really? Which department?' queried North.

The DCI avoided his eyes. 'Ministry of Defence, I'm told.'

'So there's nothing in his background to link him with St Oliver?'

The DCI hesitated.

'It's just in case the Lord Chancellor asks,' added North innocently. 'I need to have all the answers.'

Young rubbed his chin and invited the MP to sit down. 'Perhaps we'd better talk, but on an off-the-record basis,' he offered. North pretended not to understand, prompting the detective to give a further explanation. 'Byng was not, er, entirely ordinary. His job in the Lords was a post-retirement sinecure . . . After he had left the Security Service.'

'So Byng had been an MI5 officer,' said North, as though he was hearing the disclosure for the first time.

'I don't know exactly what kind of work he was doing, but it's possible he may have had dealings with both Strelets and St Oliver. I've put in a request to Special Branch for the details and I hope to hear soon. I'm not sure it's at all relevant, but it's best you know if you're going to brief the Lord Chancellor. However, you can definitely say that at present I have no reason to think his former employment has anything to do with St Oliver's murder.'

'So it's a coincidence, is it, that a probable Soviet agent is bumped off by a molehunter, with Strelets lurking close by?'

The DCI looked uncomfortable. 'Put like that, I

know it sounds odd, but we don't know that Strelets wasn't exactly where he said he was, in the Press Gallery. As for Byng's former occupation, it's immaterial. We have heard from two sources that Byng was deeply affected by the way his daughter died. I think he had every right to be. In my opinion he was acting as an enraged father, not a spycatcher. Anyway, I really don't see you have to discuss any of this with the Lord Chancellor. Ministers hate hearing about the funnies. They prefer not to know.'

'Ministers don't usually have to deal with murders,' replied North. 'As an official of the House of Lords, Byng is the Lord Chancellor's responsibility. Even if I don't volunteer the information, he's bound to find out that his librarian was a retired spook. He probably knows already.'

'Well, it's in your hands,' said Young with resignation. 'Just try not to stir up a hornet's nest, and keep the speculation to a minimum. I really think we ought to keep this exercise on the books to ourselves. If you tell the Lord Chancellor he may think this case isn't ready to be closed.'

'And you think it is?'

'That's my view,' replied the detective firmly, as Inspector Shawcross strode purposefully into the room with a small plastic evidence bag which he handed to Young.

'This was in Byng's desk,' he explained. 'I'm sorry for the delay but we had to wait for the head librarian to come in and open the desk for us. I think there's a good chance it's the murder weapon. I haven't opened it but there are traces of something brown along the top of the hasp, and it could be dried blood.'

The DCI examined the jack-knife through the plastic. He reckoned it was about five inches long, with what looked like a single blade. 'This should go to the lab straight away,' he ordered. 'Have you anything else?'

'No word from the search team at Primrose Hill and nothing from forensics on the clothes taken last night. The librarian is waiting to speak to you in the Lords Library.'

'Fine. I'll see him now,' said the detective to his subordinate before turning to the MP. 'Do you still want us to look at all these books?' North nodded in response, almost apologetically.

'Very well,' said the detective to Shawcross. 'Can you arrange it with the SOCO team to lift any prints they can from the books on the first eight shelves, and have comparisons made with Byng's prints which you can take off the body. All the books have plastic covers so it shouldn't be too difficult.'

Shawcross made a note on his pad. 'By the way, the librarian in the Lords is a she, sir. And she's very upset.'

Young nodded an acknowledgement and asked the MP if he wanted to see her too. The younger man replied that he would be along in a moment. As soon as the DCI was out of earshot, he asked Shawcross what had happened the previous evening.

'It was a flaming disaster,' said the Inspector. 'Byng is usually collected by a specially ordered radio cab when the Lords rises. There's a single call that goes out and about twenty cabs descend on the car-park. It's the same for the Commons staff, but they use New Palace Yard. Byng's taxi arrived, waited, but left without him. The DCI went crazy. A very discreet search of the Lords was organized by a team of uniformed officers at one in the morning, but Byng had disappeared. When he hadn't showed up at home by two, we all thought he had jumped into the Thames. We weren't exactly surprised when we got the call this morning.'

'But nobody looked in here?' asked North, his disbelief perceptible.

'The chief had only asked for the Lords to be searched. Nor was it intended to be particularly thorough. It would take a week to conduct a really effective search in the entire building . . . We just wanted to see if Byng was still working in the library. Don't let on to the DCI; he was up all night waiting for Byng and he's livid.' Glancing up at the shelves, he asked, 'Anyway, why are the books to be dusted?'

'I wanted to see Byng's preference in books,' replied North as he hurried towards the Oriel Room in an attempt to catch up with Young. When he reached the Lords Library, the DCI was engaged in conversation with a middle-aged woman who had been crying. She was still dabbing at her eyes with her handkerchief. On the far side of the room two men in police overalls were dismantling a desk and putting the drawers into plastic bags.

'And were you on duty with Mr Byng two days ago,

on the afternoon Lord St Oliver died?' asked the detective.

'I was,' she said, 'but I couldn't tell you about his movements. He was in and out all day. We all were.'

'Why would he leave the library?' asked the DCI.

'We all do, all the time,' she replied. 'We each have our own specialities, and sometimes we have to find a book in another part of the building. There's a big storage area in the Victoria Tower, and all the cellars are full of Parliamentary papers.'

'Would Mr Byng have had any reason to go to the Commons Library?'

'Quite often,' she said. 'Our own collection is on our computer, but the Commons Library is entirely separate. Occasionally they have a book we don't have, and vice versa.'

'So a Member of the Lords can borrow a book from the Commons,' observed Young.

'Not quite,' corrected the librarian. 'Technically, the book is loaned to us, and we pass it on to the Member. Of course, if the peer is a former Member of the Commons, he doesn't have to go through us. He can use all the Commons facilities, and borrow direct.'

Young digested the information. 'But you can't think of any reason why Mr Byng should have gone into the Commons Library late last night?'

'None whatever. I really can't believe he's dead. He was his normal self when I saw him, which was just before supper. He was working on a research request for one of the Members.'

'Do you know which one?' asked Young.

'Not unless I see the papers on his desk. But I can pull up his book requests on the computer if you like.'

'What will that tell us?'

'There's a record of book loans in his name, and requests for particular titles made over the past three months. If a Member asks for a book we don't have, and the Commons doesn't have it on its shelves, we circulate a request to the biggest departmental libraries. Then we trawl the Westminster City Library and further afield until we find it. The reader is then notified. The computer also produces a weekly list of books overdue for return. The programme works on a quarterly cycle so you can retrieve data up to three months old.'

The DCI was clearly losing interest. 'Was there anything odd about Mr Byng's behaviour yesterday. Anything out of the ordinary, however trivial?'

'He was obviously shocked, as we all were, by Lord St Oliver's death, and we talked about it over coffee yesterday morning, but he wasn't anxious or depressed, or anything like that.'

'Do you recall what he said about St Oliver?'

'Nothing rude, I can assure you. Lord St Oliver was always very courteous to the staff here. He was also good for business. He had a funny habit of ordering books he had published. It was a sort of standing joke in the library. We always thought it was his way of boosting sales.'

'Because you arranged to buy a copy?'

'If a Member requests a new book we usually add the title to our acquisitions list. I order a copy if I think it will be of interest to other Members. I think we've got all the Truscott & Sweeting books.'

'So St Oliver was quite popular with the library staff?'

'He was often in here, and he occasionally asked for *Hansard* reports from the Commons and made other small requests to the Home Affairs research section. When my colleague comes in this morning he will be able to tell you more. St Oliver concentrated on penal policy.'

The DCI refrained from making a cheap crack and closed his notepad, thanking the librarian for her help, and exchanging glances with North. 'Have you heard enough?' he asked, and turned away, moving further into the library while the MP, embarrassed by Young's attitude, continued the conversation a little longer, expressing his concern at the death of her colleague, and hearing a little more about him. After a few moments, the subject became too painful for her and she made her apologies and turned away, wanting to be solitary in her grief.

The MP thought for a few moments and then strolled after the detective, who was absorbed by a teletext news monitor. 'Nothing on the wires, yet, thank God,' he said as he heard the MP approach. 'Any ideas?'

'I have only one comment to make,' said North, still seething with anger at the DCI's treatment of the librarian. 'If you had spent a career as a professional intelligence officer, and you committed a serious crime, would you leave the evidence in your desk?

Look over there,' he said, pointing to the huge windows and the Thames beyond. 'If that knife was the murder weapon, why didn't he chuck it into the river?'

Young slumped into a large armchair nearby. 'Philip, you simply don't understand,' he said patronizingly. 'Just because someone is an intelligence officer, it doesn't mean he's super-intelligent. Most criminals are rather thick, which helps us to catch them. And even if Byng was a genius, you overlook an important factor. Many murderers want to be caught. They know they have offended, and they either confess immediately or wait until their conscience takes them to a police station. We get people coming in off the street to admit to unsolved crimes years later. You can't begin to rationalize the criminal mind, especially if it's only got a toehold on sanity. Byng probably wanted to be caught.'

'If that's right, why didn't he leave a suicide note?' demanded the MP. 'I'm not at all convinced by this, and I'm going to convey my doubts to the Lord Chancellor.'

'That's another myth,' observed the DCI. 'Not all suicides leave suicide notes.'

'Oh, really?' answered North. 'And how many people crippled with polio do you know who choose to climb up ladders to hang themselves? Byng wore a leg brace. He couldn't cope with ladders. The river, maybe . . . Under a tube train, possibly. An overdose, OK, but up a ladder, never. That's the verdict.'

Chapter Ten

Black Rod

The Lord Chancellor had spent the morning in Cabinet at Number Ten, and then had stayed for lunch with the Prime Minister. When he finally returned to preside over the proceedings in the Lords he was too busy to see North, so the MP delivered a hand-written note to his private office. In it he made an extraordinary request, but one that had the reluctant support of Detective Chief Inspector Young. The MP asked the Lord Chancellor to bring all the interviewees in the St Oliver inquiry to the Lords, so that they could each be confronted with the others, and, where appropriate, be invited to explain the inconsistencies in their accounts of the murder.

For the DCI to have backed North was remarkable, but he had been given little choice when the Home Office pathologist's preliminary report indicated that Byng's death may not have been suicide. Asphyxiation by equal pressure on the windpipe caused by the curtain sash found wrapped tightly around Byng's neck would have resulted in exactly the bruising and contusions that had been found on the body but it left unexplained two pressure marks in front which marked where his windpipe had been effectively crushed. In the pathologist's opinion, Byng might have been on the verge of death, gasping for breath, when the sash tightened around his neck. It was this element of ambiguity that made Young accept that Byng may not have died by his own hand. As well as recording the injuries to Byng's neck, the report noted that childhood polio had withered his left leg, which thereafter had been supported by a heavy steel brace.

Flummoxed, the DCI had considered for the first time that Byng may not have been a murderer, but was perhaps the victim of an exceptionally ruthless and dangerous killer who had attempted to conceal his own crime by passing the blame onto the hapless Byng. What other explanation was there for the discovery of the murder weapon in the drawer of Byng's desk? The pathologist had confirmed that the dimensions of the blade were compatible with the wounds suffered by St Oliver, and the laboratory had declared the stains on the knife to be traces of dried human blood which matched St Oliver's type. A further DNA test would determine whether the sample was identical or not.

Certainly, as the DCI had pointed out to the MP, there was no credible forensic evidence of a murder in the library room. No prints had been lifted off the wooden ladder, but that was only to be expected. Nor had Byng's fingerprints been found on any of the books that had been dusted during the previous afternoon. Two hundred volumes had been removed to the laboratory and each had undergone meticulous scrutiny. As the detective had predicted, the plastic library covers had proved an excellent environment for the preservation of prints, but Byng's were found on none of them. Far from being dismayed by the news, North almost appeared to have expected it, and it strengthened his conviction that the librarian had been the victim of an extraordinarily cunning individual.

For much of the night North stayed in the Lords Library, continuously scrolling through the computer record, making notes of particular book titles, in an attempt to reconstruct Byng's activities over the past three months.

As his investigations progressed, North became increasingly confident that he had identified St Oliver's killer, but he felt handicapped by his lack of proof. Indeed, he was still uncertain about what he thought might have been the killer's motive. He knew that if he failed, the inquiry, which had already started to wind down, would have to begin again, re-interviewing all those who were known to have been in the Lords at the time of St Oliver's death. In logistic terms, with the examination of St Oliver's bank and financial records only in the very first stage, the task ahead promised to be both long and daunting. Yet, as North was only too painfully aware, the Lord Chancellor wanted a swift and conclusive result.

When the Lord Chancellor had given his consent to

North's proposal, he had insisted that the meeting be chaired by Black Rod, the retired admiral in knee breeches who was not only a symbol of authority but also bore direct responsibility for everything that affected the security of the Lords. Although sceptical of his methodology, the DCI had agreed to the MP's idea. He felt that at worst it would waste an afternoon, at best it might help find an elusive killer, if indeed there was one. He was not totally convinced of North's theory, or his approach, but he was reassured that the proceedings would be subject to Parliamentary privilege, so the outcome of any subsequent criminal trial would not be prejudiced by the MP.

The chosen venue was the Cholmondeley Room, a banqueting suite beside the House of Lords terrace which was usually the attractive setting for formal lunches and dinners. Black Rod had exercised his considerable authority to ensure that the gathering was undisturbed, and two Doorkeepers were stationed outside to keep away the uninvited. As soon as the Lord Chancellor had issued the summons, Young and Shawcross had supervised the assignment of uniformed and CID officers to each of the interviewees so they could be escorted back to the Palace of Westminster. Reactions to the 'invitation' varied from downright hostility, manifested by Viscount Aldworth who'd finally found a friend to put up bail and had been removed from a bath in his flat in Cheyne Walk, and the Marquess of Inchkenneth, who had been on a charter to the Isle of Wight, to a more genuine spirit of co-operation showed by Viktor Strelets and Tony Rendell. The Earl of Hardington had complained that the Lord Chancellor's request was inconvenient but he, like the Duke of Hexton, had received the customary writ of summons from him at the beginning of the session and therefore knew where their duty lay. Fortunately Susie St Oliver, about whom both Young and North had expressed some worry, had agreed to attend on condition she was accompanied by her solicitor, a request that was easily accommodated as David Simons was also on the list. The Bishop had been collected by car from his cottage in Gloucestershire, and Lord Staveley had volunteered to return to London by train from his home in Cambridge. For Laurie Cox, Lady Gresham, and the Lords Librarian, attendance had meant no inconvenience, or so they had asserted. Even Maisie St Oliver, who had the furthest to travel from Leeds, expressed a willingness to participate, despite her aversion to air travel.

There was only one surprise appearance as the interviewees took their places in the sun-drenched room, chairs having been arranged in a semi-circle before a long trestle table. Madeleine Franks, who had returned to London the previous morning from Deauville, had responded to the message left for her at the Berkeley and had made no objection when North had suggested that she too come to the Lords. As she had said, when accepting what had been presented as an invitation, she had not known Sigi as a peer, so she had never been to the Lords.

As Black Rod's invited guests took their seats,

North noticed Charles Hardington avoid any contact
with Susie St Oliver and turn to Laurie Cox, whereas
Tony Rendell was positively enthusiastic in the
warmth of his welcome for Madeleine Franks who
was, as he had rightly said, exceptionally well pre-
served. She was elegant in a salmon pink suit and a
dark blue cashmere shawl and seemed delighted to
be introduced to the Duke of Hexton. Somewhat to the
Bishop's embarrassment, Viktor Strelets had engaged
him in smalltalk, and Laurie Cox had gravitated
towards Hardington. Inchkenneth and Aldworth sat
beside each other, while Maisie looked completely out
of her depth, demanding to know from one of the
uniformed officers who was in charge.

At exactly five to four the Gentleman Usher of the
Black Rod entered the room, having absented himself
from the small box beside the Woolsack where he had
just participated in the creation and introduction of a
new peer. Convention required him to entertain the
new baron to tea in the Tea Room, accompanied by
his three supporters and the Somerset Herald, and a
mere murder inquiry was not in his judgement suf-
ficient reason to break with tradition. Accordingly he
was some twenty minutes late, by which time nerves
were becoming strained and the smalltalk of those
present had been exhausted.

As soon as Black Rod took his place at the centre
of the main table, flanked by Young and North, he
introduced them and explained the purpose of the
meeting. 'The Lord High Chancellor has required your
presence here this afternoon to assist the House of

Lords authorities in bringing to justice the person or persons responsible for the homicide of His Lordship,' he said grandly. 'Your attendance is appreciated, and I am commanded to inform you that nothing which passes here will be used elsewhere in a court of law. You should therefore be entirely candid when you reply to questions put to you, but no one present is to be granted any immunity. Indeed, the purpose of this gathering is to identify whoever killed Lord St Oliver. I will now hand you over to Philip North MP, who has acted as the Lord Chancellor's personal representative in the murder inquiry.'

North rose and thanked Black Rod while he shuffled his notes. 'Four days ago, as you know, Lord St Oliver was brutally killed just outside the chamber of the House of Lords, in the middle of the debate on the War Crimes Bill. The task confronting the police has been particularly onerous, partly because so many of his acquaintances had good reason to dislike St Oliver, but mainly because of the rather public place where he met his death. The investigation has been further complicated by some deliberate attempts to obfuscate the facts. All of you present this afternoon have been interviewed by the police, but there remain some outstanding issues that have to be addressed. If I say anything that is factually incorrect, please don't hesitate to interrupt. Our intention is to find the truth.'

North glanced at Susie St Oliver and Maisie. They were sitting at opposite ends of the line of chairs, but the pained expressions on their faces showed their distaste for the proceedings. They had not come to the House of Lords to hear a diatribe against Sigi, and North wondered who would be the first to walk out. The uniformed constable at the door had instructions to prevent all attempts at premature departures. North suspected that any mention of Susie's exact status would bring a vocal response from both her and her solicitor, who was taking notes of everything said.

'Although the media have given wide coverage to the circumstances of Lord St Oliver's murder,' he continued, 'very little has been announced regarding the death in the very early hours of yesterday morning of a House of Lords librarian, Michael Byng. This gentleman had been a suspect in the original murder inquiry because he believed, with some justification, that his daughter had been raped by St Oliver. She was a young student and had been taken to one of the parties St Oliver was in the habit of throwing at his rented home in the country. After her terrible ordeal she committed suicide in circumstances that put her friend Viscount Aldworth into a difficult position, because he acted foolishly and assisted in the destruction of her suicide letter, which would have ensured that St Oliver did not escape punishment for his conduct.'

Susie and her solicitor had exchanged several glances and North realized that he had reached the limit. Maisie also looked as though she was on the brink of breaking down. As for Jonti, he looked positively radiant, fully aware of how damaging North's

statement could have been in relation to his own contribution to Leander's death.

'The other person affected by the death of Michael
Byng's daughter was His Grace the Duke of Hexton,
who was very attached to her, and this he readily
explained to the investigation.' North stole a look at
the Duke, who seemed nonplussed by the comment.
'The police had intended to interview Mr Byng on the
night he died, in an effort to eliminate him from the
inquiry, but he was found dead in the House of
Commons Library.

'The police are now satisfied that although Mr
Byng's death was intended to look like suicide, it was
in fact a coldly calculated murder. I have been asked
not to divulge the exact nature of the evidence, but it
is compelling, even to a layman like myself. In fact
the murderer made a serious miscalculation.'
Although not entirely true, the DCI had suggested
this unsupportable claim in the hope of catching the
killer off-guard, but North suspected it was really
intended to enhance the diminishing reputation of the
inquiry. Whatever Young's purpose, North had acqui-
esced to the suggestion.

'What I can tell you is that the murder weapon
used to kill Lord St Oliver was found in Mr Byng's
desk, almost directly above us, in the House of Lords
Library. Accordingly, two possibilities arise: either
Michael Byng murdered Lord St Oliver, and was
killed by another person entirely, someone who had
nothing to do with St Oliver's death; or, as is much
more likely, Byng was murdered by St Oliver's killer.

The first scenario implies the existence in the Lords of two killers. On statistical grounds alone, I am advised that we can discount this interpretation, at least for the time being.

'Let us take the second scenario, and look at how Mr Byng found himself in the Commons Library. I think we can assume that although there were not very many people around so late, after the Commons had adjourned for the night, he either accompanied his killer to the particular room in the library, or he met the killer there by prior arrangement. Either way, we can deduce that the murderer was entitled to be there. The murderer would not have wished to be challenged on the way either to or from the scene of the murder, and the Badge Messengers, the police officers on patrol and the security staff have been especially vigilant over the past few days. On that basis it is safe to assume that Byng knew the murderer, who was almost certainly allowed to enter the House of Lords Library as of right. We can, I think, discard any idea that Mr Byng was the type of person who would assist in smuggling an unauthorized person into the Commons Library, in contravention of the very tight security regulations that had governed his life for the past twenty-five years.' This was North's only coded concession to what he now knew to be Byng's former career as an MI5 molehunter. 'Using those criteria, the field is really very small because the Commons Library is accessible only to the library staff, officers of the House, current Members of the Commons and former Members who are now in the Lords.

'The only peer present today who fits that description is Lord Rendell, but he told me when I questioned him on this issue that he had not met Mr Byng, and that he rarely uses the library.'

'That's quite accurate,' responded Rendell, suddenly paying more attention to the proceedings.

'Doorkeepers,' continued the MP, 'can only be distinguished from their counterparts in the Commons, the Badge Messengers, by experts, as they wear the same white tie and tails. Only their badge of office is different. I doubt whether Members of the Lords or Commons know that, and they are to be seen circulating everywhere in the Palace of Westminster. Indeed, one of their duties is to carry duplicate telephone messages to the respective Members and they routinely enter almost every room in the building. They are blind and deaf in terms of the proceedings that they encounter, and they are renowned for their discretion. They patrol up and down the corridors, slip into committee rooms and search the restaurants and bars for their quarry, catching the eye of a Member for whom they have a message. It's a highly efficient service but it means that they have become part of the scenery. They're hardly noticed, and a Doorkeeper might easily have entrapped Mr Byng in the Commons Library, perhaps by seeking his help on a book, or even arranging by telephone to meet him there at a particular time.'

Laurie Cox could take no more. 'I'm sorry for interrupting, sir, but this is all wrong. No Doorkeeper would attack a Member or an official of the House. It's quite impossible.'

North nodded in agreement. 'The Badge Messengers and Doorkeepers are the guardians of this establishment, and it would be a sad day if one of this ancient and honourable group of men betrayed the trust bestowed upon him. But the fact remains that you were one of the first on the scene when St Oliver was murdered, and you certainly have the physique to lift Mr Byng on to the ladder where he was found. If you did kill Mr Byng, I'm at a loss to understand why, unless perhaps you suspected that Lord Hardington with whom you served in the Royal Marines, was really the murderer. It's my belief that you thought Hardington was the culprit because you certainly lied to protect him when you denied having seen anyone in the Not Content Lobby. I think the Earl came up from the rifle range and you saw him. Your first instinct was to help the officer who had once commanded you. If so, perhaps you can tell us where you were the night before last?' asked the MP.

'It was my night off. I was at a dinner at the Special Forces Club,' said Cox. 'I probably stayed until midnight, and then I went straight home. I've plenty of witnesses. I did serve with His Lordship in the Marines, but I was telling the truth when I told you that I had not seen anyone in the lobby. I really didn't.'

'Very well,' continued North, undeterred by Cox's alibi. 'We will have to return to Lord Rendell. We only have your word for it that you didn't know Michael Byng, and you've reiterated that statement, but it can't be true. According to the computer records of

titles lent to you over the past three months, you have
had a long interest in the subject of Second World
War intelligence operations, but more recently you
have been loaned several rather obscure text books
on cryptography.'

'You forget I am a military historian,' replied
Rendell. 'I borrowed plenty of books from the library
while I was working on my biography of Sir Desmond
Morton, but I took the books home with me. I've never
worked in the library.'

'And you don't know Michael Byng, another military
historian?' asked the MP, his disbelief apparent to all.

'What's he written?' asked the peer.

'*The Salerno Mutiny*,' replied North.

'I may have heard of it, but I certainly didn't connect it with a librarian in the Lords. It may be that
Mr Byng handled my book requests, but I'm sure I've
never met him.'

'That's curious,' replied North. 'It was only when I
noticed last night, while examining Mr Byng's computer files, that just a fortnight ago you borrowed a
book entitled *MI9*. It was then that I realized you
must have killed Michael Byng. Although it was
loaned to you and returned on time by you, and
Michael Byng had handled your request, no fingerprints were found on the book. Now that struck me
as distinctly odd. All the other books in the military
history section, which were examined individually by
forensic experts, were covered in very clear fingerprints. Yet someone had deliberately removed all trace
of prints from *MI9*. Now we have to ask ourselves,

why should somebody do that? Only two people could conceivably have a motive for doing such a thing: Michael Byng, perhaps to conceal the fact he had touched the book, and you, for the same reason. But Byng is dead, and there is an entry in his library computer showing the book loan. If he had wanted to destroy any connection between himself and the book, for whatever reason, however improbable, he would have deleted the entry on the computer, but he didn't. Which means you must have wiped the book clean. Why?'

'I'm not saying another word,' said Rendell, visibly shaken. 'You tell me. I've never heard of anyone being pilloried because their fingerprints *weren't* at the scene of a crime. It's really too fanciful. Go on, tell me.'

'I'll try,' responded North. 'The first question is, why should anyone have wanted to kill Michael Byng? There are no obvious reasons, especially if he didn't murder Lord St Oliver. And why was he killed before he spoke to the police? Perhaps the timing of his death was significant. I think he knew something that would identify St Oliver's killer. Obviously it was not something that on its own made it clear to Byng that the person concerned was a murderer, or he would have alerted the police and taken the appropriate precautions. He certainly wouldn't have risked meeting him alone, in a deserted room late at night. So it must have been some innocuous item of information that, once imparted to the police, would have led them directly to Lord Rendell. So here's the conundrum. What was it that compelled Rendell to kill Byng? I've racked my brains over this, because I now realize I was the one who, quite unintentionally, indicated to Rendell that Byng was a suspect and was due to be interviewed. I accidentally tipped him off because I trusted him to tell me what he knew about Byng. We had a short chat in the Members' Lobby and when he denied knowing him I thought nothing of it, but I think my chance remark threw Rendell into a panic. If so, it suggests that Rendell had been completely ignorant of the connection between St Oliver and Byng. It also means that Lord Rendell *never expected Byng to be a murder suspect in the St Oliver case*, and when the unthinkable happened, and he did become one, His Lordship decided to turn a desperate situation to his advantage.

'We must now ask ourselves, what was the innocuous but inconvenient fact known to Byng that so endangered Rendell? As Byng was a librarian, and his murder occurred in the library, one might justifiably conclude that it concerns books, or a particular book. My attention has concentrated on the single book Rendell is known to have borrowed, which is also the only one he was so determined to wipe clean. What is so special about *MI9*? Rendell has been loaned several of the books from the military history section over the past few months, but this is the only one that is entirely devoid of fingerprints, so it *must* have, or have had, some special significance for him. Unfortunately, fingerprints can't be dated, so there's no way of knowing exactly when they were left, or when they were cleaned off. And what makes the whole thing so odd is that no attempt has been made to remove the computer record of the loan, so either the murderer didn't realize there was a computer record, or the fact that the loan had occurred didn't itself really matter. Perhaps the murderer was anxious about that book that night? Did they discuss it, and did they both touch it when they met? That is definitely possible, because the Lords Library doesn't have a copy of *MI9*, so every time a peer wants to borrow it, a request is made to the librarians in the Commons.

'Let's return to those fingerprints for a moment. Imagine for a moment Rendell has arranged to meet Byng in the library, at a particular time, to discuss something to do with the book. They're both military historians, so there could be any amount of pretexts available as a purpose for making the rendezvous. Byng has retrieved the book from the shelf, and he hands it to Lord Rendell, so the fingerprints of both are on it. Rendell murders Byng, cleans the book cover, and replaces it in the shelf. Presumably he has realized that to leave the book out, for the police to find, would be to provide a clue that pointed to himself as the murderer, but is that right? Others have borrowed the book too. So is there something in the book which quite categorically links Lord Rendell to Lord St Oliver?

'The name of neither appears in the index, and I've read the book twice without spotting the St Oliver connection. It's an account of the wartime allied escape and evasion service and the ingenious methods used by MI9 to help prisoners of war to escape from

Axis prison camps. Now here there is a very vague link. It's well known that Lord Rendell's father was a fighter pilot who was killed in the war when his son was just a boy. But when I checked on his death notice, it stated very clearly that he died while on active service. He wasn't killed in action, and that's an important distinction. Tony Rendell's father was a prisoner of war. Furthermore, he was one of the fighter pilots sent to Russia to train Soviet aircrew on the Eastern Front, and when he was shot down in 1943 he was kept as a prisoner in German-occupied Lithuania.

'As almost every reader of the tabloids knows, Lord St Oliver was Lithuanian in origin, and he came to this country as a refugee after the war. What is rather less well known is St Oliver's true name. When he arrived in England he was known as Sigismund Rosenbaum, and he anglicized his surname to Rose. However, according to Viktor Strelets, who has spent some time researching St Oliver's antecedents, Rosenbaum was not his real name either. Sigismund Rosenbaum was born Yacov Orobinsky. Naturally, I checked both names in the index of *MI9*, but neither appears. Yet I'm convinced that there's something in that book that is the key to Byng's murder. There must have been something about the book that would have made Byng realize that Rendell had killed St Oliver. If not, he'd be alive today.'

'This is all ridiculous speculation,' protested Rendell. 'None of this amounts to a shred of proof. It's laughable. It's all supposition.'

'It's more than supposition,' countered North. 'From the moment that Lord Rendell told me, in an aside, the exact date when the law was changed that the House of Lords would no longer sit in judgement upon peers, I suspected that he had taken more than a passing interest in the fate that would befall St Oliver's murderer if he was caught. When we originally interviewed him, Lord Rendell implicated two people: Lady Gresham, who had once been close to Lord St Oliver, and the Earl of Hardington. With characteristic style and subtlety, Lord Rendell correctly pointed out that the Earl had lost a considerable fortune as a result of his partnership with St Oliver in their publishing venture. He implied, rather disingenuously, that Hardington was enormously wealthy, and so therefore he was an improbable suspect. But he must have known that we would soon learn that Hardington faces ruin as a result of his involvement with St Oliver. So by his deliberate assertion that Hardington's great wealth excluded him as a suspect, Rendell was actually taking care to compromise the Earl while simultaneously putting himself in the clear. After all, everyone knows that Lord Rendell is extremely wealthy.

'The matter of Rendell's motive is a real puzzle, and I admit to being mystified. As he had delicately pointed out, he's too rich to worry about the minor inconvenience St Oliver has caused him financially. So why did he kill St Oliver? I only began to discover the truth yesterday when Madeleine Franks returned from Deauville. Note that she had been staying in

Normandy, and not in Antibes where Rendell had told the police she had gone.'

'A slip of the tongue,' suggested Rendell.

'I doubt it,' said North contemptuously. 'For some reason you were anxious that we shouldn't speak to Miss Franks who was, of course, married to Lord St Oliver when he was plain Sigi Rose. What was it that Miss Franks could tell the police that was not so significant that it might put her life in danger, in the same way that Michael Byng had been eliminated, but might compromise Rendell? Miss Franks and Lord Rendell dined together at a party at Mosimann's a week or so ago, and during the course of the evening the conversation turned to mothers. Madeleine Franks was sure that she had told Rendell that when she had been married to Sigi Rose he had tried to persuade the Soviet authorities to let his mother leave the country. Although she could recall few of the details, because it had all happened so long ago, she remembered very clearly telling Rendell that St Oliver's name at birth had been Orobinsky. I believe that it was that single, apparently innocent remark that transformed the fun-loving Lord Rendell, who hitherto had been so content to spend so much time with St Oliver, and have his books published by him, into an enraged murderer. The realization that St Oliver was really Orobinsky sent Rendell into a homicidal fury, and compelled him to cut the old man's throat. I also think that the link between Orobinsky, Rendell and St Oliver lies in that book, *MI9*.'

'I think I may be of some assistance here,' offered

Lord Staveley, who had been following North's remarks with scholarly care. 'There is a very significant disclosure in *MI9* that may be relevant. I remember because I reviewed it for the *Spectator*. The book was not allowed to be published until 1979 because it contained an important secret. It revealed how, during the war, Allied prisoners were briefed before they went into combat on what they could expect if they were captured. One crucial aspect of the course was the communications part, when selected men destined for the front-line, and therefore in danger of being taken prisoner, were taught a simple code with which they could send secret messages to the War Office. The Geneva Convention entitled all PoWs to post letters home through the Red Cross, via a neutral power, and upon their arrival in London they were examined by MI9 to see if the letters contained a secret message. It was a terribly simple system, which was its attraction. If a prisoner dated his letter in a particular way, with numerals interspersed with strokes of the pen, instead of the more usual English convention of spelling out the month in full, and if he underlined his signature too, it was a signal that the text concealed a code. The full length of the message was obtained by counting the letters of the first two words after the normal salutation of 'Dear Mother', or whatever was appropriate, and then multiplying them together. The code itself was straightforward substitution, and although the texts took a long time to construct, the PoWs had no shortage of that particular commodity. It meant that if a letter began 'Ghastly food', for example, it meant that there was a message of twenty-eight letters hidden in the text. This was quite a revelation at the time, as I recall.

'Naturally, when that disclosure was made, many relatives who had treasured their correspondence from their menfolk in the camps, especially those that didn't return home, were scrutinized to see if they had hidden messages. Quite a few slipped past the War Office examiners, and it's my guess that my noble Lord Rendell made such a discovery. I think that you'll find that either he or his mother kept his late father's letters and it was only when he read *MI9* that he realized his father, whom presumably he had hardly known, may have inserted something into the text. If we look at those letters, I'll bet one of them has something to say about a Nazi called Yacov Orobinsky.'

'And that would explain Rendell's recent interest in cryptography,' said DCI Young. 'Having found the signs indicating there were hidden messages he started to study codes and ciphers. It also gives Rendell a motive for keeping the police away from Miss Franks, and wanting to silence Byng. Only Miss Franks could confirm that Rendell had taken an interest in someone called Orobinsky and wartime codes. Taken separately, they are meaningless, innocuous facts. When put together, they identify Rendell as a man with a very convincing motive for murder.'

'I take it all back,' said Rendell slowly. 'I always thought Bill Staveley was just an old bore, but I was mistaken. Congratulations. You've almost got it right. I expect you'll search my house and find the letters anyway, whatever I say, so I may as well tell you. Orobinsky was a monster. A five-star, twenty-four-carat authentic monster. I don't think he was a mass-murderer, or anything like that, but he was deeply, deeply evil. Orobinsky was one of the SS guards at the hospital where, after my father was shot down near Kiev, he had both his legs amputated. He was terribly burned, but he might have survived, he had a chance. Instead, the last days of his life were made a hell by a guard who was determined to prove to the rest of his squad that he was even more cruel than them. My mother received three letters from Flight Lieutenant Lord Rendell, but she never realized that in them he had identified the location of his camp on the Baltic, and had named the guard who had tormented him as Yacov Orobinsky.

'St Oliver was a truly despicable human being who didn't deserve to live,' he continued. 'You really can't imagine the pain my father must have endured before he died, and you will never understand how I felt about St Oliver once I had made my discovery. When you read the code inside the letters, you will see that I have done nothing more than execute my father's last, dying wish. What more can a son do?'

'And what about Byng?'

'Do you know, we met only once. I would telephone him with my book requests, or send them to the library through the internal post, and the books would appear the next day at the loans desk where I would sign for them. During all that time, we never spoke face to face. If we had, I would have realized he was crippled and couldn't manage a ladder . . . And I would have had to think of something else.'

'But if you never met, what danger did he present to you?'

'Unlike my son, who is entirely computer literate, I am not. Mr Byng mentioned that if I had a particular subject in mind, or a person, he could access a history database which would produce book notations for each reference. At the time I had asked his advice about books on the SS and the war in the Baltic, and naturally I seized the opportunity to enter the name Orobinsky. There was no trace, but I knew that the police would be bound to delve into St Oliver's background, and they would find out that he had once been called Yacov Orobinsky. This wouldn't matter, so long as Byng was not interviewed by the police and asked about that same name. If he was, he'd immediately think of me. When Philip North told me that Byng had suddenly become an important suspect, I knew he would connect me to the murder. Without that link, there was absolutely no motive that could be attributed to me.'

'So you arranged to see Byng?' asked the DCI.

'I telephoned him and said I had been having difficulty finding *MI9* on the shelves and asked him to come over to the Commons Library and show me. He was too polite to suggest I trouble one of the Commons librarians, and came straightaway. Because he had not yet seen the police, he had no reason to be suspicious of me, and I did what was necessary. It was only when I met him that I saw he was terribly crippled, and my plan to attach his body to the ladder proved much more difficult than I had anticipated. Then I wiped the book that we'd both handled free of fingerprints. I had originally decided to drop the knife into his pocket, but that seemed too suspicious. Instead I went to the Lords Library and slipped the knife into his desk.'

'But if you had never seen him, how did you know which was his desk?' asked North.

'I used the fax machine at the end of the room and dialled his extension. As soon as I heard the telephone ring once, I had identified his desk. The rest was simple. My intention was to divert attention away from the Lords. If Byng was a principal suspect, and he hadn't seen the police, there was a chance his death would end the investigation.'

'It nearly did,' replied the MP quietly.

More Compelling Fiction from Headline:

MURDER IN THE COMMONS
A PARLIAMENTARY WHODUNNIT

NIGEL WEST

'A JOLLY, OLD-FASHIONED ROMP, WELL-CRAFTED
AND FULL OF INSIDER INFO' *THE TIMES*

'MPs dread only one thing more than turning
up in Nigel West's pastiche whodunnit – and
that is being left out' *Today*

When an unpopular Labour MP is killed in front of the
House of Commons, the Speaker asks Philip North,
Conservative MP and the victim's pair, to liaise with the
detectives in charge of the case. But even North is
surprised when the apparent hit-and-run incident is
revealed to be a complex murder investigation in which
there are plenty of suspects: the jealous secretary, the
ambitious ex-wife, the drunken back-bencher, the
frightened mistress and the sinister constituency agent ...

As North digs deeper to expose carefully hidden secrets,
the lobby correspondents smell corruption, the whips
fear scandal and a government minister anticipates
accusations of treason.

Praise for MURDER IN THE COMMONS:
'A fiendishly complicated murder story' *Sunday Express*
'He is at his convincing best' *Mail on Sunday*
'Solidly crafted plot, but main fascination lies in insider's
exposure of parliamentary anachronisms and how 's
your father' *The Sunday Times*

FICTION/CRIME   0 7472 4176 7

TAKEOUT DOUBLE

A CASSIE SWANN MYSTERY

SUSAN MOODY

Two years of teaching biology had been enough.
Two years of dissecting frogs and reeking of
formaldehyde had finally persuaded Cassie Swann
to set up as a bridge professional instead. So far, she
has managed to make a reasonable living, operating
from her Cotswold cottage.

And then, during a Winter Bridge Weekend at a
country-house hotel, she finds three of her punters
dead around the green-baize table. And at least one
of them is indisputably the victim of murder.

Nothing to do with Cassie – or is it?

When she realises that her livelihood is now
threatened by the unwanted notoriety, she is forced
to undertake some investigations of her own.

Set amid the eccentricities of English village life,
Takeout Double is the first in a marvellous series
featuring an amateur sleuth in the obsessive world
of bridge players.

FICTION/CRIME   0 7472 3946 0

KATE CHARLES

Appointed to Die

A clerical mystery

**Death at the Deanery – sudden and unnatural death.
Someone should have seen it coming.**

Even before Stuart Latimer arrives as the new Dean of Malbury
Cathedral shock waves reverberate around the tightly knit
Cathedral Close, heralding sweeping changes in a community
that is not open to change. And the reality is worse than the
expectation. The Dean's naked ambition and ruthless behaviour
alienate everyone in the Chapter: the Canons, gentle John
Kingsley, vague Rupert Greenwood, pompous Philip Thetford,
and Subdean Arthur Bridges-ffrench, a traditionalist who
resists change most strongly of all.

Financial jiggery-pokery, clandestine meetings, malicious
gossip, and several people who see more than they ought to: a
potent mix. But who could foresee that the mistrust and even
hatred within the Cathedral Close would spill over into
violence and death? Canon Kingsley's daughter Lucy draws in
her lover David Middleton-Brown, against his better
judgement, and together they probe the surprising secrets of a
self-contained world where nothing is what it seems.

A selection of bestsellers from Headline

APPOINTED TO DIE	Kate Charles	£4.99 ☐
SIX FOOT UNDER	Katherine John	£4.99 ☐
TAKEOUT DOUBLE	Susan Moody	£4.99 ☐
POISON FOR THE PRINCE	Elizabeth Eyre	£4.99 ☐
THE HORSE YOU CAME IN ON	Martha Grimes	£5.99 ☐
DEADLY ADMIRER	Christine Green	£4.99 ☐
A SUDDEN FEARFUL DEATH	Anne Perry	£5.99 ☐
THE ASSASSIN IN THE GREENWOOD	P C Doherty	£4.99 ☐
KATWALK	Karen Kijewski	£4.50 ☐
THE ENVY OF THE STRANGER	Caroline Graham	£4.99 ☐
WHERE OLD BONES LIE	Ann Granger	£4.99 ☐
BONE IDLE	Staynes & Storey	£4.99 ☐
MISSING PERSON	Frances Ferguson	£4.99 ☐

All Headline books are available at your local bookshop or newsagent, or can be ordered direct from the publisher. Just tick the titles you want and fill in the form below. Prices and availability subject to change without notice.

Headline Book Publishing, Cash Sales Department, Bookpoint, 39 Milton Park, Abingdon, OXON, OX14 4TD, UK. If you have a credit card you may order by telephone – 0235 400400.

Please enclose a cheque or postal order made payable to Bookpoint Ltd to the value of the cover price and allow the following for postage and packing:
UK & BFPO: £1.00 for the first book, 50p for the second book and 30p for each additional book ordered up to a maximum charge of £3.00.
OVERSEAS & EIRE: £2.00 for the first book, £1.00 for the second book and 50p for each additional book.

Name ....

Address ....

....

....

If you would prefer to pay by credit card, please complete:
Please debit my Visa/Access/Diner's Card/American Express (delete as applicable) card no:

Signature .... Expiry Date ....